Praise for

Nikki McCoy

…you've got everything needed for an interesting story. I look forward to the next release. ~ *Literary Nymphs Reviews*

Total-E-Bound Publishing books by Nikki McCoy:

Everything That You Are

Keepers of the Gods
Son of Death

Keepers of the Gods

SON OF DEATH

NIKKI McCOY

Son of Death
ISBN # 978-0-85715-732-4
©Copyright Nikki McCoy 2011
Cover Art by Posh Gosh ©Copyright 2011
Interior text design by Claire Siemaszkiewicz
Total-E-Bound Publishing

Published in 2011 by Total-E-Bound Publishing, Think Tank, Ruston Way,
Lincoln, LN6 7FL, United Kingdom.

Total-E-Bound Publishing is an imprint of Total-E-Ntwined Limited.

Manufactured in the USA.

SON OF DEATH

Dedication

To my mom, who never gave up hope, my children for being the joys (and banes) of my existence, and my husband...who makes every precious moment of my life a miracle.

Chapter One

As soon as Jamie heard the spray of water hitting tiles in the bathroom next to their room, he sprang into action. It was a short trip to the kitchen where he filled and started the coffee machine, then prepared two mugs with just the right amount of sugar and cream.

Theirs was a small house, but shabby by no means. The kitchen was almost as large as the living room, and while that wasn't saying much, they managed to keep them both free of clutter. This gave their home a cosy atmosphere instead of inducing the claustrophobia one would expect to feel in such small spaces.

There were two bedrooms — one they shared, and one which had been deemed Jamie's office, although that was more of a title than a fact. A jumbled collection of decorations and household items that Loland had accumulated over his years as an interior decorator reigned supreme.

Every week, Jamie was forced to clear a path to his work station, consisting of a worn pine desk, chair, computer and fax machine, but he didn't mind. He loved to imagine the kinds of homes that would eventually house each piece as he was working.

Jamie returned to their bedroom and began to rifle through the clothes inhabiting Loland's side of the closet. Most of them had either designer tags or were close knock-offs. The significance of the names on the material went right over his head but he knew it was important to his partner.

He'd also been keeping tabs on the outfits Loland wore on his dates with his boyfriend. He knew exactly which shirt to match with which pants to give Loland a fresh look every time he went out.

It had been odd at first, helping his lover prepare to meet another man. No other Dom Loland had met had ever had him this flustered. For that matter, no other man had piqued Loland's interest enough for him to want to engage in more than just casual scenes at the club. Jamie knew this one was special. The energy Loland gave off following each date was sizzling with love and lust, and somehow it only enhanced their own relationship.

Loland had informed him that this was another actual date, not a club rendezvous, so Jamie decided on a pair of dark grey slacks and a long-sleeved, white button-up shirt that shimmered even in dull light. After laying the clothes neatly on the bed so as not to wrinkle them, he went in search of Loland's watch, cell phone, and wallet, lying in various places throughout the room, and lined them all up on the dresser.

He warily eyed his lover's vast shoe collection and was tempted to pick out a pair to save Loland the hassle of having to choose, but he remembered the one time he'd made that mistake. Instead of the usual ten minutes it took for Loland to decide on his footwear, it had taken the man forty minutes to find the perfect outfit to match the shoes Jamie had chosen for him. That had been for the first date and since then Jamie had taken the liberty of dressing the man himself.

Not willing to go there again, Jamie instead walked to the living room and found a jacket for Loland that would go with his outfit and be appropriate for the weather outside. A peek out of the closed blinds covering the window showed that it was going to be a clear, if chilly, night. The perfect opportunity for Loland to try out the new lightweight leather long-coat he'd unearthed at Sears while shopping for a client.

With nothing left to do, Jamie retreated to the kitchen, poured coffee into both mugs, and sipped at his while waiting for the entertainment to start.

It didn't take long. Two minutes later, he heard the shower turn off and watched with a bemused expression as Loland ran to the kitchen, dripping water everywhere, with only a hastily wrapped towel around his narrow hips.

"So I was thinking of wearing my blue sweater, but I don't have any..."

"Bed." Jamie pointed to their room and watched the taller man scramble in that direction. He heard a muffled, "Thanks," and waited patiently for the rest of the ritual to play out.

Loland came hopping out on one foot, trying to walk and put on his trousers at the same time. "Have you seen my..."

"Dresser."

The man hopped back into the room then reappeared five minutes later, asking, "Is that coffee I smell?"

Jamie handed him the second mug still sitting on the counter and tried to stifle his laugh as he watched his lover accept it with glee. Watching Loland enjoy a good cup of coffee was like watching a man in the throes of the best orgasm of his life. It never got old, and it was always as sexy as hell.

His prick swelled to life at the sound of Loland's little added moans thrown in for extra effect. Jamie had to tighten his grip on his own cup to keep from grabbing Loland and swallowing those sounds in a thorough kiss. The quick peck on the mouth Loland gave him didn't help matters at all. Loland raced back to the bedroom while Jamie took a seat on the couch.

"So he's taking me to that new Benihana restaurant they opened up in Paradise Valley," Loland yelled from down the hallway. "I can't imagine how he got reservations there on such short notice. I heard there was a two-month waiting list to get in and that was weeks before they even opened their doors."

"Well, you have been seeing him for three months."

"Yeah, but that was just casual hook-ups at the club. This is our sixth date. It takes us to a whole new level on the relationship scale. Chukka or Memphis?"

"Memphis." Jamie grimaced at the ease with which he had replied. He tried his best to avoid the fashion world like the plague. The fact that he could now make decisions on which style of shoe would fit an outfit best without even looking at them did not bode well for him. "So, you really like this guy, huh?"

It was a needless question. Loland constantly spoke of the man's looks and actions with adoration. His past was still a bit of a mystery, but at this point, Jamie felt as though he knew him almost as well as did Loland.

Truthfully, he sounded like the kind of guy Jamie could fall for as well.

But that would never happen.

"Yes," Loland said as he came out and plopped himself down on the couch next to him. "And I know you'll love him too. He has the cutest little dimple on his left cheek when he smiles and have I mentioned his ass? Oh man, I could go on for..."

"Wait, wait, wait. What do you mean 'I'll love him too'? He's your boyfriend, not mine." Jamie could feel the familiar sense of panic begin to rise and take root in his chest. He tried to hide the panic he knew was shining in his eyes, but Loland must have noticed before he could cover his face with his hair.

Loland reached out and placed a finger under his chin, then gently began to kiss him — the corners of his mouth, his nose, his eyebrows, the lines creasing his forehead. "I wouldn't introduce you to anyone that would hurt you, baby. I've been a lot more careful since...well, since last time. You're the most important person in the world to me. You know that right?"

Jamie finally looked up through his lashes and met Loland's sincere gaze. There was not a hint of deception or anger to be seen in those soft brown eyes. There never was. He could feel the waves of bright, pure energy rolling into him from the other man that attested to his honesty. He didn't want to rehash the reasons why it would be a disaster for him to meet any of Loland's friends. There was no need to ruin his lover's excitement for the evening.

"I know. And I know what happened before wasn't your fault." He decided to lighten the mood by kissing Loland's mouth and grasping the bulge between his legs in a firm grip. He rarely let his aggressive side show, but every time he did, it was the perfect distraction. Loland gasped and swivelled his hips, silently begging Jamie to rub along his growing erection.

Jamie pushed forwards until his slighter frame was resting atop Loland's across the couch. He ground his hard-on into the crevice between his lover's cock and hipbone. The fabric of his jeans wasn't kind to his sensitive flesh, but the friction felt amazing. He delved his tongue into Loland's mouth and reached up to tweak his nipple with his other hand. Jamie was rewarded with another gasp and a fresh wave of sexual energy.

He nudged copper curls aside with his nose as he kissed his way down his lover's jaw and found the erotic spot just beneath his ear. He bit into the soft flesh above Loland's collarbone and gave the head of his cock a tight squeeze at the same time, drawing out loud pants and whimpers.

The power of taking control always hit him with a rush. It was what Loland needed, and what Jamie desired most in the world to give to him, but he could only keep up this act for so long. As much as he longed to be everything to his partner, he was no dominant.

With more than a little reluctance, he slowly eased back into his true submissive nature and whispered against Loland's lips, "You're going to be late." The dazed look in Loland's eyes almost made him change his mind about releasing him so he could go on his date. The temptation was there, clawing at him as it always did when Loland went out, but he knew that there were things the man needed that Jamie couldn't give to him.

"I can stay home, baby. If you want to spend some time together, I'm all for that. Or I can take you with me. I know he wouldn't mind. We could skip the fancy restaurant and go somewhere private. It would be just the…"

"No. I love you and I'm telling you to go on this date. I can see that this one makes you happy." Jamie quickly kissed away the protest he could see building on the thinning lips of his lover. Loland would probably let him get away with murder in his bid to make him happy in any way that he could, and Jamie did his best not to take advantage of that through his own selfishness. Loland needed to be dominated just as much as he did. He could tell by the satisfied haze his lover had been floating around in for the past several months that the man he was seeing met his needs.

"Go. Meet this guy, then come home to me so hot and horny you have to drill me through the mattress just to take the edge off." Jamie knew he'd finally lessened his lover's worries when Loland threw his head back and laughed. The sound reached into his soul and cleansed all of his worries about being left alone again in their small home for the night.

"Okay. Are you working a shift tonight?" Loland asked.

"Yea, but only a half one. I should be done by the time you get back."

Loland stood up and straightened his clothes before donning his leather coat. "Do I look all right? Thank you for helping, by the way. Don't know what I'd do without you."

"You're welcome, and you look great. My sexy top. Now go have fun. I have annoying people to piss off."

Loland chuckled as he leant down to give Jamie a chaste kiss, then headed for the front door. "Lock this. Keep your cell phone on you, and call me if anything happens, or even if you just need me to come home for…whatever. I'll be back soon. Promise me you'll call if anything happens."

Jamie tried his hardest not to roll his eyes as the second part of their ritual played out. Loland had always been protective of him. Ever since the episode with the last man Loland had taken an interest in, his lover had become obsessively fussy.

It had taken him over six months to convince the man that he would be fine on his own. He may still get panic attacks and work extra hours just to keep the paralysing fear at bay, but there was no way Jamie was going to let Loland know about that. The man had already sacrificed enough for him.

"Yes, Sir. I promise."

Loland paused in the doorway and bit his lip. The indecision on his face was somehow endearing and exasperating all at once. Jamie wanted to scream at him that he was wiser now. He could take care of himself. But at the same time, he was afraid of losing that special concern that no one else had for him. Loland was his ray of sunshine in a life soured by the ruthless desires of other people. He was a gift that Jamie would never take for granted.

He stood up from the couch and swung his hips in a sultry sway as he approached Loland. In a soft, seductive voice, he said, "I swear to be a good boy until you get home. After that, I promise nothing." Loland groaned into his mouth as Jamie stole another kiss. Their lips met in a bruising clash and Jamie clamped his fingers around the hard sides of his lover's waist. He borrowed confidence from Loland's solid frame and poured as much assurance into his voice as he could muster.

"I'll be fine. Enjoy yourself."

Loland gave him one last kiss before closing the door behind him. Jamie swiftly locked both deadbolts and secured the chain on top. With the added security they had installed into their new home, he felt some relief from the ever-present fear that continuously threatened to steal the fragile hold he had on his self-control. The succour was tenuous at best, and he mentally repeated his mantra of solitude all the way to his office. *Loland is strong. Loland is smart. Loland will keep me safe.* Of course, when Loland said it, it always came out as, *"You are strong. You are smart. You will stay safe for me,"* but no matter how hard he tried, he couldn't instil the same amount of faith in himself that his partner apparently had in him.

And what the hell was up with his notion that Jamie should meet his new Dom?

Loland and Jamie had always shared an open relationship. Well, open on Loland's end. But the inviolable rules in their partnership clearly stated that Jamie was, under no circumstances, required to meet the men his lover dated.

The factor of jealousy was not an issue. Even Jamie couldn't deny that he desired the kind of domination Loland described in his relationships with men he called 'Masters' at the clubs he frequented. However, never once before tonight had his lover alluded to an inclination for Jamie to meet whoever was Loland's Dom at the time.

A wave of anguish swept through him as he imagined the humiliation his lover would endure if he brought over his boyfriend. Jamie was awkward at best, with skin so pale he could pass for a ghost due to his reluctance to go outside. His raven-coloured hair didn't help matters, and he was far from muscular...or tall...or even toned.

Truthfully, he had no idea what Loland saw in him, or why the man bothered to keep a lover action-packed with issues. But he wasn't about to tempt fate by embarrassing him in front of a guy Loland was obviously taken with. Then there was always the compounded concerns of his powers. If the guy was slotted to die soon, Jamie would know. And what if his precognition kicked in, giving him a glimpse into the man's future that Loland might not be happy with?

He wouldn't be able to hide his reaction, and the thought of lying to his lover made him queasy. Honesty was imperative in their relationship. Loland had been the first and only person to believe that his powers were real and not a figment of his imagination. He could never betray that trust.

No. When it came down to it, there was no other option. He could not meet this man. His power of precog had taken mercy on him a few weeks after Loland had started seeing his boyfriend, once given the assurance that this guy would make Loland happy. He'd never told Lo about it, but maybe he should. It would ease his lover's mind. But for now, he had Internet complications to tackle.

Chapter Two

Seth walked slowly to the centre of his garden, inhaling the wild fragrances of the lush vegetation that surrounded him. His little slice of paradise was cordoned off from the rest of his back yard by a circle of willow trees that each stood at a good height of at least fifteen feet. A cherry wood fence lined the perimeter, covered in flowering vines, lending additional privacy along the base of the trunks.

The inside of his sanctuary had been designed by himself and a Feng Shui artist who was also a fellow Keeper. He had not the slightest talent for landscape design or the symmetry of natural art, but the Keeper had insisted that the garden be built according to Seth's personal balance, taking into account that with which he desired to surround himself. The consultations and decision-making had taken longer than the actual construction, but it had all been worth it. More than worth it.

A fountain composed of stacked slabs of obsidian rock represented the focal point in the centre. From there, a circular path of smaller, rose-coloured flagstones added to the hardscape element and continuously wrapped around until the path ended at the door to his kitchen.

The softscape had been intricately engineered to complement the hardscape without overwhelming it. The overall effect gave one the impression that the beauty of Mother Nature could easily overpower the designs of man, but instead, she chose to blend with them in harmony.

His anticipation over sharing this with his new-found mate caused little sparks of electricity to dance upon his skin, licking and teasing until he was forced to rein it in. He couldn't afford to lose his focus while giving obeisance to his gods.

He stopped just before the little pond ringing the fountain and raised his arms out from his sides while leaning his head back to greet the night sky. He allowed the energy he had collected over the past few weeks to coalesce inside him and prepared to release it into the realm above, when a soft voice brought him to an abrupt halt.

"Seth, my dear. You have become a fount of energy over the past few months. Not that I'm complaining, but many of us are curious as to what, or who, has caused this change within you."

Seth opened his eyes to see the Goddess of Fate sitting demurely on the stone bench to his right, resting atop a bed of perennials and lilacs. He lowered his arms and turned to face her corporeal form, resisting the urge to pat himself on the back for withholding his sneer of contempt.

"I'm sure you already know the answer to that, no thanks to you. If not for the Goddess of Love, I would have missed my opportunity to meet him that night at the club. What are you here for?" Seth allowed the suspicion he felt at presence of the Goddess seep into his eyes, letting her know that he was aware of her schemes, if not her actual plans behind them.

He'd not forgotten the sudden urge that had overcome him to leave the BDSM club he had been visiting the night he'd met Loland. Since his job as a trainer of Keepers was directly intertwined with Fate, he was well accustomed to the feel of her power. That had been a betrayal of not only his fate, but the Goddess' very providence as well.

It was her main responsibility to guide Keepers to their mates. So many of his kind were driven to despair or isolation without the balancing effect of the love of a mate. The work she commissioned him for was secondary compared to the importance of finding that one person who could relieve the insufferable solitude he was forced to endure. Seth had existed for centuries, patiently awaiting the mate who could bring him peace in his bleak yet tumultuous world.

Recalling how close he'd come to missing his chance to unite with the man brought his anger over that night to the forefront. Only the small interference of the Goddess of Love had saved him from what could have been the most disastrous night of his long life. Her method of causing Loland to become the object of desire among a group of lustful Doms may not have been the most ideal, but it had created the perfect distraction.

His need to protect the smaller man had superceded his nearly uncontrollable compulsion to vacate the premises. Loland's initial shock at the rash of heated advances of every Dom within a twenty foot radius of him would have been comical if not for the blinding fit of jealousy Seth had experienced. Fortunately, he had been able to rescue the sexy bottom before the unwanted groping had turned into unforgiveable acts of lewdness.

"Just because your mate is close does not always mean it is the most opportune time to meet her, or him, in your case," Fate snapped. "Besides, I still don't know why you insist on trifling with men when there are so many gorgeous women in the world."

"Like yourself, for example?"

Fate let out an inelegant snort. "Oh please. My level of existence is far superior to that of the mere mortals who inhabit this earth, as you well know. The offer still stands, by the way. You know I can make you much happier than any of these pathetic humans."

This time, it was Seth's turn to grunt stiffly. Been there, done that. Once upon a time, Fate's illustrious golden countenance had appealed to him on a primal level. Through her manipulations, they had transgressed in a secret tryst, back when he had just come into his duties as a Keeper.

The affair had been a whirlwind of lust, passion and fornication. To this day, he had no regrets about their torrid fling. It had been the deciding factor on the inner conflict he'd held on whether or not he was gay, and it had also been enough to disenchant him with Fate's wiles.

While he loathed the Goddess now more than he ever would have thought possible, he still could not bring himself to show outright disgust for one of his deities. "State your purpose, Goddess. I have plans with my mate tonight that I do not wish to delay any further."

"Yes, about that. I have a new recruit that will need your services as of tonight. He's located in Fairbanks, Alaska. Your flight leaves at eleven o'clock, so I suggest you start packing now."

Raw anger surged through his body, threatening to take over the last vestiges of his control. The energy he had yet to release raced like fire through his veins, revving his adrenaline to dangerous heights. Through gritted teeth, he replied, "Then I'll be taking the one after that. My priority now is my mate. The training I do as a *favour* to you can wait."

A flush of blood stained her cheeks in what would have been a becoming pink if not for the unflattering spite sparkling from her blue eyes. She gave a very juvenile huff and asked, "Am I to assume, then, that you would leave a fledgeling to his own lacking devices simply because you can't control your libido?"

Seth threw back his head and let out an exasperated burst of laughter. He refused to negotiate his happiness with a Goddess who was indebted to him for the services he rendered instead of the other way around. "Believe what you want. I don't give a shit! If the boy is in such dire need of being trained immediately, I'm sure Aquene would be more than happy to lend his time and knowledge. He is the senior Keeper in that area, after all. Otherwise, I will leave no sooner than tomorrow. Take it or leave it, Fate."

She jumped up and performed a comical little two-stomp dance of frustration before relinquishing her corporeal form and returning to wherever it was the Gods spent their eternal existence. By this time, the energy still contained within his being was sizzling and spitting through the pores of his skin, making him feel like a lit sparkler on the Fourth of July.

Without his customary preamble, Seth thrust his hoard outwards to his Gods, expelling every ounce of energy he'd gathered over the past few weeks. Despite his sour mood, he couldn't help but feel the tiny surge of pride that came with the knowledge that his mate had provided roughly half of all he'd collected.

The little man was a compact bundle of bright, untainted energy that seemed to overflow onto others wherever he went. It was a good thing he had a naturally sunny disposition.

Once the last of his stock had been received by the Gods, he relaxed his posture and took a moment to centre himself. Most Keepers offered up their hoard once a week, preferring not to take the chance of succumbing to the baser nature of the type of energy they collected.

The potency of human emotions, especially the darker ones, could have disastrous effects on the minds of his kind if contained for too long. It was why so many Keepers chose to live on the outskirts of society and simply collect the energy nature provided. He, however, had centuries of discipline in dominating the flux of energy he absorbed and loved the rush it gave him when he was almost filled to capacity.

Before he'd met his mate, he had been able to withhold the energy he absorbed for as long as a month, but his little sub of sex and spunk had proven to be a test for even his vast stores of control. Trying? Yes, but oh so worth it.

After taking a minute to acclimatise himself to his now empty psyche, he turned and re-entered his house through the sliding glass doors. Seth itched for a shower even though he'd taken one prior to releasing his energy, if only to cleanse the memory of the sour meeting with Fate from his mind, but he was already running late.

Soon he would expect obedience in everything from his mate as his submissive, and it would not do for him to set a bad example. With a soft sigh of resignation, he tugged his long coat over his relaxed suit jacket and grabbed his keys from the basket on the end table next to the garage door.

The restaurant he'd chosen was an easy ten minutes away, which gave him just enough time to ponder the oddity of his mate's personal predicament. While he could be appreciative of Loland's openness when it came to the terms of their relationship, the knowledge that his destined other half was currently in love with another man posed quite a troublesome problem.

There was no question as to whether Loland would accept his role as a submissive. He seemed born to the lifestyle just as much as Seth was, but Seth knew he couldn't bring himself to collar his mate when the little man's heart held devotion for someone else. It was definitely a point of possible contention that needed to be addressed immediately.

Forcing his mate to abandon the man he loved was not an option, but neither was the possibility of settling for second place. He chuckled as he realised that, for the first time in his long life, he finally understood just how much power a human mate held, let alone a submissive. He definitely had his responsibilities as a Dom cut out for him.

Seth pulled up to the front of the restaurant and handed his keys to the valet, tipping a little extra for the expediency. Once inside, he was shown to a private table towards the back, hidden behind a cream-coloured paper partition. It allowed him a measure of privacy and was far enough away from the other customers to mute their conversations to a low buzz.

Loland was already seated and he couldn't help but mimic the slow smile that spread across his face, lighting up his handsome features. Copper strands hid one of his warm, brown eyes as he ducked his head and waited patiently for Seth to take the tall seat beside him. The familiar rush of energy from the mating pull bathed Seth in an intoxicating heat.

Their meals had been pre-ordered, but they were left alone for a time to sip at their sake. The energy Loland was emitting was surprisingly subdued, as though he was a little nervous. There was no doubt that the smaller man had a concern, but Seth decided to let him voice it on his own.

"You look very nice this evening, but then you always do. I'm beginning to think that your talent as an interior decorator also extends to your wardrobe," Seth commented with a quirked brow.

Loland flushed a deep red and lowered his chin even more so that his curls shadowed almost his whole face. From experience, Seth knew that they were just as silken in texture as they appeared, and he took the opportunity to touch them again as he raised Loland's face. "Don't ever hide this beauty from me. You should take pride in compliments. You deserve them."

The way Loland dragged the tip of his tongue across his upper lip while locking his gaze onto Seth's groin had his cock suddenly standing at attention. Damn. The man had innocence and irresistibility down to a fine art.

"Thank you, Sir, but Jamie should get most of the credit. If not for him, I'd probably still be at home, naked, with the entire contents of my closet piled up on my bed."

"Then you'll have to convey my appreciation. How is Jamie doing?" The third party in question had become a regular topic of discussion early on in their dates. Seth knew it was Loland's way of reiterating the fact that he was not willing to sacrifice his current relationship for a new one. Still, the situation had to be the oddest Seth had ever found himself in.

He was no stranger to open relationships, having partaken in them numerous times over the years. Knowing that his mate had a boyfriend at home who aided and encouraged his dates with another man was definitely a first, however.

"He's good. Working. Umm...Sir? I was wondering if I could ask you a question. About Jamie."

"Yes?" Seth could feel the desperate energy rolling off his mate, but before Loland had a chance to voice his question, two servers approached the table with sauces, dishes and wrapped silverware. The chef rolled out a trolley full of meats and vegetables and turned on the flat cooking surface in front of them.

Both he and Loland paused to watch the preparation of their meals. It wasn't the knowledge that the food was cooked fresh right in front of them, or quite the mixture of wonderful aromas wafting from the grill that never ceased to hold the diners of real Teppanyaki Asian cuisine in rapture. It was the fanfare.

Their chef held nothing back as he deftly sliced their meats and flipped each thin strip into the air to land among a bed of assorted vegetables. Liberal squirts of water and seasonings caused steam to rise in pillars, occasionally interspersed with small bursts of flame when the cook added a flare of alcohol.

The final step of placing the food onto the china plates was no less of an exercise in skill as the man artfully piled everything together to give it the appearance of colourfully ordered chaos. Seth nodded to the chef in gratitude for the man's care as he left, but his own thanks for setting up the date came in the form of a burst of raw, sexual energy.

He looked over to see stark need gleaming from the eyes of his mate. He'd never been one for flaunting his fortune to get what he wanted, but who was he to argue with the obvious, visceral reaction such a small display of wealth derived from his mate?

"I take it you're pleased with the date so far?"

"Oh yes. If Sir would allow me, I'd like to show my appreciation for everything before we eat." Loland reached out his hand and gently squeezed the head of his cock through the thin material of his pants.

Seth cast a cursory glance around them to ensure that they didn't hold the unwanted attention of any of the employees, then said, "On your knees, boy." He caught the sly grin that curved Loland's full lips as the man slid gracefully from his chair to the floor between the base of the grill and Seth's groin. He was completely hidden from sight and Seth watched as his sexy sub freed his swollen cock from the confines of his trousers.

It took all of his willpower to bite back the groan that threatened to escape as he felt the glorious heat of his mate's mouth surround his member. That sweet tongue flicked the slit on top before swirling it around the engorged head. Seth let his eyes roll back as he lowered one of his hands beneath the lip of the table and took a firm hold of the soft locks tickling along his thighs.

"Take yourself out. You will not come until I give you permission." Seth watched with half-lidded eyes as Loland hastily freed his hard prick from his pants and began to stroke himself in time to the bobbing of his head.

Public sex had always been a favourite pastime for him. Not only did he get to enjoy his own rush of excitement over the possibility of getting caught, but the jittery energy of his partner provided additional stimulus. The energy Loland gave off now was ten times the amount of his past lovers, driving Seth to almost frenetic heights of ecstasy.

Seth tightened his hold on the soft curls in his grip and forced Loland to swallow his entire length. Seth wasn't a small man. However, his mate had proven to be adept at relaxing his throat to accommodate his considerable size. Seth revelled in the power of controlling the smaller man's airflow as he kept Loland's tight lips pressed to the base of his cock.

Loland continuously contracted and released the muscles at the back of his throat while increasing the pumps of his hand on his own cock. Seth relinquished his grasp on his eager little sub to allow him to breathe, then slammed his head back down. He could feel his sac tightening as his balls pulled up against his body, preparing for his imminent climax, but he gritted his teeth in an effort to hold it back. The wonders of Loland's mouth always had him on edge and ready to spurt within minutes. He wanted to draw it out a little bit longer, though, and savour the miracle of his mate's masterful skills.

Loland inhaled heavily through his nose once he was given permission to pull away again. His boy created a rhythm of movement and suction that quickly pulled Seth back to the brink of release.

"Come, boy. Now." That was all the warning he had time to give before his orgasm shot from his balls and out of his cock with such force that a loud grunt was ripped from his lips. He used both hands to yank Loland's gifted mouth down to his pubes, giving the man no choice but to gulp down his cum until he milked him dry. The groan that vibrated along Seth's cock, signalling his mate's climax, triggered a wave of aftershocks that caused spasms to roll through his thighs and abs and centre in his groin.

It took him several moments to marshal his breathing before he was able to give one more casual glance around them. Finally releasing his crushing hold, he peered down at the man still kneeling obediently at his feet.

Any fear that he might have been too rough was dispelled as he took in the look of utter adoration on Loland's face. Seth felt his control slipping as he realised that there wasn't anything he wouldn't do to put that expression on his mate's face with every chance he got.

He grazed the pad of his thumb lightly over Loland's swollen lips, tempted to bruise them further in a demanding kiss, but he managed to tamp down his urge.

"In your seat, boy." Seth tucked himself back into his pants as Loland rose and sinuously turned his slender form around to ease back into his seat. Seth took hold of the hand that still cupped his mate's sperm and sucked each finger into his mouth, delighting in the taste of Loland's cum. To any onlookers, it would seem as though he were licking up the juices from the food Loland had yet to handle.

Loland moaned and traced the path of Seth's tongue greedily with his eyes. Seth bit down with just enough pressure on the last digit he lavished his attention on to draw Loland back to their surroundings. Afterwards, he discreetly tucked the semi-stiff length of his boy back into his pants.

"Thank you, baby. Now eat. Boys cannot subsist on cum alone." Loland gave a contradictory snort that brought out a gust of laughter from him. He reluctantly turned his attention back to his food, knowing Loland would follow suit. "So you were going to mention something about Jamie. Is everything all right?"

Loland choked slightly on the beef in his mouth but tried to hide it behind a quick swig of his drink. "Yes, Sir, umm...everything's fine. Well, actually...I, uh... I know that we've only been seeing each other for a few months now, but uh..."

Seth took note of the sudden, anxious intensity of his mate and tried to assuage his tension with touch. The brush of his hand on the underside of Loland's jaw had the desired effect and he watched the slender man take a deep breath before continuing.

"I have to go out of town in a few weeks for a job. My boss wants me to design the layout for the reception area and ballroom of a hotel opening up in Vegas. It's not my usual thing but if all goes well, I could be looking at a raise and it could bring in a range of clients from there as well as from New Mexico, California, and maybe even Colorado. I could get my name out there and possibly break off from the company to start my own some day. I don't have the resources yet but I've got the ambition, and with the publicity of this job, I could really get the ball rolling."

Seth waited patiently until Loland ran out of steam, amused by the man's animation. There was a point to his rambling tirade, he was sure, but he was in no hurry to find out what it was. Part of Loland's charm was the gestures he put with his words. He had a way of physically embellishing his stories that drew his audience in, causing people to take as much pleasure in listening to him as he took in the telling.

This was a side of his mate that he wasn't able to see when they frequented the BDSM club they'd met at. Loland had informed him that he didn't have any formal training as a submissive, and Seth couldn't wait to begin that venture, but he'd wanted to know the man before he schooled the sub.

Loland carried on for a few more minutes about the type of job he would be doing and Seth noticed that his voice seemed to rise along with his level of nervousness.

"So anyway, I know this is a little sudden but it shouldn't be too much trouble for you. I'll be back in a week and Jamie will probably drown himself in work while I'm gone. I'll be eternally in your debt and make it up to you in ways that will keep you awake at night. I was hoping we could make a pit stop at my house at the end of the night so you can meet him. I don't want to railroad him at the last moment with this. It's the first time I've left him on his own and I worry about him. So what do you say?"

Seth blinked. He didn't *think* he'd missed an entire section of that speech, but stranger things had happened. "Boy, I get the feeling you're asking me for a favour, but I think I missed something in the translation there. Care to run that by me again?"

A beautiful blush stained Loland's cheeks. "Sorry. I, uh...I meant to ask if you could keep an eye on my partner, Jamie. Check in on him from time to time while I'm gone. He hasn't been on his own since I met him years ago and he can get kind of...quirky...when left to his own devices. Not that he's incapable of taking care of himself. He's just...special. Wait, this is coming out all wrong."

Seth chuckled at Loland's sigh. "This has got to be one of the more awkward moments of my life, but I don't think your request is too much to ask for. When did you say you're leaving?"

"The seventeenth. Two weeks from now. I have to be there Monday morning for a consultation with the owner of the hotel."

Seth grimaced as he recalled the Keeper he was supposed to train in Alaska. While he was sure that

Aquene would gladly take over the task of tutoring the young man, the older Keeper had his hands and house busy with six budding kids of his own. He didn't want to burden the man with one more charge to take responsibility for.

Loland misinterpreted his expression and hurriedly said, "I'm sorry. I know this is a lot to ask for. If you feel uncomfortable, I can cancel my plans…"

"Loland, hold on. I didn't say no, but are you telling me that you would pass up the chance at a promotion because you're afraid of leaving your boyfriend home alone?" The fierce dedication shining through the hard glare of his mate's eyes gave him his answer. "Okay. I never meant to doubt you. If it means that much, then I can put off my plans until you get back. Staying here for a few more weeks sounds infinitely better that what I had scheduled anyway."

Uncertainty replaced the protectiveness on Loland's face. "You're leaving?"

Seth wasn't sure how much he could reveal about himself at this point in their relationship, but he figured he had to start somewhere. "Only for a little while. I have to…train someone. It usually takes a month or two, but it's nothing that won't keep until you get back."

"Oh wow. Now I feel like a real shit. I'm sorry to put this on you. Maybe this isn't such a good idea right now."

"Stop apologising. And don't change your plans. I'm glad I can do this to help. Now, if you want me to meet him tonight, I think you should tell me more about him. How long have you known him?"

The rest of the dinner was spent discussing Loland's mysterious boyfriend. Seth managed to keep half of his mind on the conversation, but the way Loland's pants bunched up around his crotch, outlining his generous package, made for a powerful distraction.

He also couldn't help but notice the way the man's golden, sun-kissed skin glowed in the soft, overhead lights, or the fact that the sheen from his shirt lightened his brown eyes, making them an almost perfect match to the highlights in his burnished hair. His frame was slim but nicely toned. Seth was sure the man must work out, but any hopes he'd had of getting him into bed tonight were taken away each time Jamie's name was mentioned.

No, that wasn't fair, he chastised himself. Jamie was a part of his mate's life. A huge part, apparently, and from what he could gather, this was the first time Loland was placing the man's welfare in someone else's hands. Seth wasn't about to risk failing such a leap of faith.

By the end of the meal, Loland's energy level was back to its normal, high-static frequency and Seth followed him home. This was going to be a very long, very interesting night.

Chapter Three

A cold sliver of fear raced down Jamie's spine. His eyes lost focus and his hearing was sucked into a vacuous void. His faculties shut down and all he was left with was the vision of the man about to enter his home.

He was tall and muscular, with a demanding countenance and a face that looked as unforgiving as his large, capable hands. Despite the panic threatening to overwhelm him, Jamie felt his breath hitch in his throat at the sexy, masculine beauty of this stranger. He seemed the avenging angel and cruel God all wrapped up in a hot, huge package that would have made a blind woman blush.

The vision faded just before his senses came flowing back in a rush that had him gasping for air. Shoving aside the disgust for his twisted libido, he promptly disconnected his hands-free phone, terminated his Internet connection and ran to the front door. He flipped light switches on his way, dousing the house in darkness.

Muffled voices and footsteps increased in volume on the porch and his anxiety tripled as he realised the man was not alone. *Not again. Never again.*

He grabbed the metal baseball bat from underneath the small stand beside the door and bolted silently on bare feet to the bathroom on the other side of the house. Fingers slick with sweat fumbled with the knob once he was inside until he realised that there was no lock with which to secure himself within.

Shit! He'd never got around to installing a lock on the bathroom door, and now he would face the consequences.

Violent tremors competed with choppy inhalations as he begged his body to still. He was sure the pounding of his heart would alert the trespassers to his presence regardless of whether he managed to gain control of himself or not. This time, though, he refused to go down without a fight. He'd rather die than live through the knowledge that he had once again disappointed his lover.

The sound of the locks being released on the front door and hushed voices penetrated his erratic thoughts and a buzz built behind his eardrums. He feared he would never be able to track the intruders over the roar in his head but the sound of footsteps approaching cleared his mind like nothing else. He sucked in one last gulp of air and glued his gaze to the doorknob that was slowly turning in front of him.

He didn't let the momentary blindness of the overhead light being switched on distract him. With deadly aim, he swung the bat at the head of the stranger, at least a foot above his own, and felt his bones rattle when it came to a jolting halt. For one sickening moment, he thought that he might have actually imbedded the weapon in the other man's skull when he wasn't able to pull it back. But there had been no crunch.

A sharp pain flared in his wrists as the bat was twisted from his fingers and thrown halfway down the hall. Thick arms surrounded and lifted him so that all he could do was flail his legs in a vain attempt to escape. A scream of terror was wrenched from his throat but the tight grip only increased, crushing his chest until it was all he could do to suck air into his lungs.

"Enough! I'm not going to hurt you. Calm down."

"Jamie!"

Loland's voice pierced through his fog of terror and he renewed his efforts to get away from the man holding him. It was unnecessary, however. One second he was enveloped by more strength than he'd thought one man could possess, and the next, he was discarded like a rag doll and dumped unceremoniously on his butt.

He sat, dazed, until his lover came and wrapped him in a familiar embrace, whispering words of comfort in his ear.

"Jamie, baby, this is my boyfriend, Seth. The man I wanted you to meet, remember? He... Wait." Jamie felt Loland's curls brush against his temple as his lover turned his head. "Did you just try to hit him with the bat?"

Soothing energy seeped into him until the trembling finally stopped and Loland's words went from a jumble of syllables to coherent sentences. "Boyfriend?" Pulling away from Loland, Jamie turned his head to look up at the man in question. And up. And up. He realised his position on the floor didn't give him much of a vantage point, but he was going to sprain his neck trying to take in the full height of the guy. "Lo, I don't think that's a man. He's more like a bear. Polar size. Maybe grizzly."

He quickly clamped his mouth shut. What the hell was wrong with him? First he mistook the man for an intruder and tried to cave in his skull, now he was insulting him.

So much for a good first impression. At this rate, Loland was likely to kick him out by morning if there wasn't any chance of salvaging his relationship with this bear. *Man!* Long night. Very long night.

As Loland stood up, Jamie scrambled to hide behind his back.

"Jamie, honey, it's okay. He's big but he's nice. I'm very proud of you for defending yourself. Relieved that no one got hurt, but proud just the same. Are you going to come out from behind me and say hello?"

"Uh-uh."

A deep, rumbling chuckle filled the small confines of the room and Jamie peeked wide eyes over the top of Loland's shoulder. The large man had a smile on his face that diminished some of the fierceness his frame imposed, but not enough to make Jamie feel comfortable around him. There was an odd look in his gaze as he raked it blatantly up and down what he could see of Jamie's body, as though he were shocked by his very presence. That couldn't be, though.

"It's all right, boy. Why don't you two go put some coffee on while I finish taking care of business, then I'll join you."

Loland nodded and turned to leave, but Jamie stubbornly held on to the back of his shirt, keeping him between himself and the hulking beast. Once the door blocked off his view of Seth, Jamie felt his muscles turn to jelly and was grateful for the support of Loland's arms as he was steered into the kitchen. Loland was laughing at him, but he didn't find the situation particularly amusing.

"I'm sorry. I only saw him coming. My vision didn't include you. Lo, I'm really sorry. I didn't mean to ruin your date."

"It's not your fault, baby." Loland began to put on the coffee and either chose to ignore the fact that Jamie was shadowing him or realised he needed that closeness. "I should have warned you that I was going to bring him over. It's just that, well, there's something we need to discuss, but I want to wait for Seth to be here."

Jamie's thoughts spiralled into a cyclone of apprehension and his heart plummeted to his stomach. If there had been anything in it, he was sure it would have come up at those words. As it was, he was able to force away the temptation to dry heave, but not the cold sweat that once again broke out over his body.

"You're getting rid of me? Lo, please. I promise I won't be stupid again. I'll…"

Loland grabbed him by the shoulders and gave him a little shake. "Jamie, what are you talking about?"

"You're leaving. I can feel it." And he could. He wasn't always struck by a vision when his power wanted to play. Sometimes, he just *knew* things.

"And what have I told you about drawing conclusions based on the information that your power gives you? I'm glad that you guarded yourself when you saw Seth coming, but I think when it comes to me, I deserve a little more credit."

Loland was right. The impression he got over the loss of his lover did not carry the oppressing weight of a permanent break. But the break was there, nonetheless.

"I don't understand."

Loland sighed, then the towering build of the stranger filled the frame of the entryway to the kitchen, cutting off their conversation. A ripple of electricity shot down Jamie's spine and went straight to his dick. There was something magnetising about the man that he hadn't noticed before. It called to him, and he barely caught himself from walking over to get closer to the alluring energy he exuded.

Jamie watched as his partner strode across the room to plant a kiss on the man's lips and guide him to a chair before returning to pour coffee into the cups he'd prepared. Even sitting, the giant seemed to dominate the room.

Jamie felt a peculiar shift in the flow of energy around him. It felt as though it were being manipulated by an unseen force, but he was too preoccupied with putting as much distance between himself and the stranger as possible to dwell on it. The appalling attraction he felt towards him was as confusing as it was embarrassing.

Dark silver eyes softened as Loland brought Seth's mug to him. A strong current of something unidentifiable yet familiar passed between them as their fingers touched. The brief, heated glance they shared was reminiscent of the kind that Loland gave to him on occasion. Is that what love looked like? Jamie stared at the look of pleasure on Loland's face as his lover walked back to the counter, and tried desperately to remember if he had ever incited such strong emotion in his partner.

Suddenly, he felt as if he were the intruder here. Between the time Loland had left for his date and his return, the rules had somehow changed and he was no longer certain of where he stood. Loland handed him a cup but instead of following him, Jamie slid away until his back met the far counter. A quick glance at the stranger let him know that his retreat had not gone unnoticed. Loland took a seat at the table across from the bear and drew in a deep breath.

"I have to go to Las Vegas for a job. The original decorator backed out and my boss thought of me to fill his spot. I won't be leaving for a couple of weeks and I'll only be gone for one. Seth has agreed to help out here if you need anything. I'll never be more than a phone call away and he only lives..." Loland cast a perplexed glance at Seth. "I've never been to your house, have I?"

"We can rectify that this weekend. All of us, so that Jamie will know where to find me if he needs to. I'm only about twenty minutes away."

"Okay, that sounds good. Jamie, what do you think?"

What did he think? There was no possible way to answer that without the conversation ending in an argument. The idea of being on his own was terrifying, but Loland's career was everything to him. Demanding that he sacrifice such an obviously important job would be selfish. If he accepted Seth's offer of help, he would be admitting that he needed a babysitter, and that was just too humiliating to contemplate. If he refused it, Loland might change his mind about going which would, again, put him in the doghouse.

He was sure he could stock up on groceries to last him a week so that he wouldn't need to leave the house, but what if there was an emergency? Venturing out amongst crowds was even more daunting than being alone.

He chewed at his lip until he tasted the sharp tang of blood. They were both staring intensely at him, awaiting his answer, and he was surprised to find that Seth's expression mirrored Loland's. It was full of anticipation, as though he were just as anxious for him to agree with the plan as Loland was. Jamie couldn't imagine why. Who in their right mind would get excited over coddling a twenty-two year old man who should be able to control his own fear?

Well, he had to grow up sometime. "I'm glad you got the opportunity, Sir. I think you should go, but Seth doesn't have to watch over me. I can take care of myself."

The doubt painted on Loland's face was definitely a blow to the ego, but it was Seth who replied first.

"Jamie, there's no shame in asking a friend to come over to see how you're doing or keep you company for a little while. Usually, that's what family is for, but Loland's informed me that neither of you have any here. I also think this is a great opportunity for us to get to know each other better. I have a feeling we'll be seeing a lot more of one another in the future."

Was that desire he saw in the man's eyes? No, it couldn't be. If it were, Jamie would have felt the same revulsion he always did when any man but Loland looked at him in hunger. Instead, there was just more of the sizzling electricity that danced along his skin like butterflies.

Jamie didn't miss the appreciative look Loland sent Seth at his words. Loland's energy calmed dramatically, as though his nervousness had been alleviated by the confidence in Seth's voice. There was love between them. It was plain to see, even without the benefit of his precog.

A weight settled in Jamie's chest, but instead of the jealousy or abandonment he had expected to feel knowing this day would come, he only felt an inescapable sense of acceptance.

Loland needed a top, just as Jamie need Lo to be his top. Sharing his lover didn't matter. So long as the man was still willing to love him, nothing else mattered. What was one week compared to Loland's happiness?

"I can do this on my own, but I guess…I could get to know you."

Loland burst from his chair and proceeded to squeeze the life out of him in an excited hug. The gush of energy Jamie felt from him attested to his happiness, pulling a smile from Jamie despite his misgivings.

"Thank you, sweetheart. You know I just want you safe, right?"

"I know. Look, I, uh... I ended my shift early so I'm going to call it a night. Will you...be coming to bed soon?" He flicked his gaze to Seth but the man's face revealed none of his emotions.

His previous insecurity crept back into him. This was the first time Loland had ever brought a man home to meet him. Jamie wasn't sure whether he had a right to make demands on Loland's time or if he should wait until Loland came to him. It was selfish, but he wanted to spend as much time as possible with his lover before he left.

As if reading his thoughts, Loland answered, "Sure. I want to spend the next few weeks with my baby. Besides, we'll be seeing Seth tomorrow. Let me just show him out and I'll be right behind you."

Oh yes. How could he have forgotten the trip to Seth's house so that he could learn where the man lived, in case he had a psychotic breakdown or something? He. Couldn't. Wait. They both turned at Seth's low chuckle and, as soon as Jamie locked eyes with him, the man raised a single, knowing eyebrow at him. Apparently his mind was an open book tonight. He might as well broadcast his emotions on the Internet for all that his skill at subtlety helped him.

Sighing, he trudged to their bedroom and hoped that his mind would take mercy on him and settle, allowing him to sleep eventually.

* * * *

Later that night, Seth returned to his garden, but this time it wasn't to expend the energy he'd collected or to take solace in his private refuge. He had a major bone to pick with the one Goddess who could give him the answers he needed.

It wasn't often that he, or any Keeper for that matter, summoned the Gods. It was an ability they all held but rarely had a use for. However, because of the service they provided, the Gods had no choice but to answer when called upon.

After taking a minute — or five — to control his seething emotions, he tilted his head back and splayed his arms, opening himself up while chanting the name of the Goddess he wished to speak to. It didn't take long for Fate to appear at her customary perch on the bench beside the fountain. Seth's anger shot up another few degrees at her audacity to look perturbed at being called upon.

"Am I to believe this is a purely social call or did you really miss me that much?"

Seth bit back the retort scalding the tip of his tongue. At one point in time, he had enjoyed her flirtatious demeanour. The quips back and forth had been a challenge and he had perfected his skills of seduction with her as a sparring partner. That had quickly ended when she realised their affair would not progress beyond their one night of passion.

Even if she had the right equipment, Seth would never have entered into the relationship she'd so desperately wanted. Lust had turned to spite, and he'd already suspected that had something to do with her effort to divert him from discovering his mate, but this time she had gone too far.

"What the hell is going on, Fate? First you try to keep me from my mate, now this."

"Excuse me? I have no idea what you're talking about, and even if I did, you can't take that tone of voice with me."

"The fuck I can't. He's had no guidance, no training. He's already so damaged he can barely leave his house. Why?"

"I have no idea to whom you are referring," Fate hissed.

"My second mate!"

Fate's face paled to a sickly white and Seth noticed the slight tremor in her hands as she reached up to wipe the fine sheen of sweat glistening on her upper lip. "That can't be. He's supposed to be dead."

She whispered it so quietly that he knew she hadn't meant him to overhear, but he was so attuned to her now in his rage that she might as well have shouted it.

"Dead? As in murder, fatal accident, spontaneous combustion, what?"

Fate sputtered as she tried to regain her composure. It wasn't a pretty sight and he was in no mood to give her time to bat her ridiculously long lashes while she thought of a convenient lie.

"Fate, you will tell me now." He used his Master voice and was grimly satisfied to see that it had the same effect on her that it had on mortals and others of his kind.

"I, um, I saw that he was fated to die years ago. I didn't want you to have to go through the pain of losing one mate when you still had another out there."

Wow. He'd underestimated her ability to come up with a lie in five seconds or less. That would have actually been conceivable from a vindictive brat like her, but for one tiny detail.

"You and I both know that if he were fated to die, Death would have taken him. The God makes allowances for no one, and no one has ever escaped your notice before, either. Tell me, Goddess, how it is that a Keeper destined to die years ago is still running around without your knowledge?"

Fate's colour changed from pale to a spectacularly unflattering shade of green and her lips compressed into a thin line. "I have to go."

"Oh, no you don't." Seth lunged at her but she was gone by the time his arms wrapped around the empty space left in her wake. "Fate!"

The fury that consumed him was too much for his body to handle alone. Sparks of energy from the surrounding plant life surged into him and swirled into a tightly coiled flurry of heat and force until he'd become no less than a living conduit of power. It cleansed and renewed in a blazing rush before erupting out of his chest and into the night in a dazzling display of light and crashing sound.

The explosion left him feeling weak and drained, but his mind was racing. His simple question to Fate had produced a myriad of others, each one more unsettling than the last. The only bright spot in this whole mess was the fact that he'd found his second mate and had the perfect excuse to get to know him while keeping him safe.

Of course, that looked to be a challenge in and of itself. If what Fate had hinted at about Jamie's death was true…

Seth knew he would stop at nothing to keep Jamie alive, whether the man wanted his help or not. Rising to his full height, he surveyed the damage from his outburst. The trees had fared well, but many of the bushes and flowers were wilted and drooping, their energy stores depleted. Thankfully, it was nothing that he couldn't fix within a week or so.

Back inside the house, he walked to his study and pulled up Aquene's phone number from his Rolodex. His long-time friend may have chosen the wilds of Alaska for a home, but his notorious social skills were just what Seth needed right now. The man had an uncanny knack for gaining information from even the most stubborn Gods due to his 'charm'.

On the third ring, he noticed the time and grimaced. Three o'clock in the morning was pushing it, but Aquene answered before he could hang up.

"Someone better be dead, dying, or signing up to train all six of my boys."

Well, at least he could make a fair trade for the task he was about to ask the man to undertake. "I'll take option three, but only if I can maim them when they get out of line."

"Seth? Is that you? You know, for a friend that hasn't contacted me in over a year, you sure got lousy timing. Me and the wife were just working on number seven."

Seth bit back the urge to laugh at that. Last he'd heard, Aquene's wife had threatened to kill him if he got her pregnant again. "My apologies, old man. I know it's late, or early in your case, but I have a situation that requires your unique brand of expertise."

"Is this serious enough for me to get away with demanding payment in the form of option three?"

"Absolutely."

"Then lay it on me, brother."

"Well, I found my mates."

"Really? Congratulations!" Aquene boomed. Seth snatched the phone a good foot away from him before the man blew out his eardrum in his excitement. "That's wonderful! See, I told you it would...oof. Cheryl, Seth finally found his mate, can you believe...oof!" There was a short pause then Aquene came back on the line. "One sec, man. Gotta move to the living room. Apparently good news in this house can only be taken during the day."

This time Seth did chuckle. It was actually fortunate that Aquene's mate had kicked him out of their bedroom for this conversation. Once the realisation that Seth had used the word 'mates' instead of 'mate' hit him, Aquene's volume was sure to rise even higher. He kept the phone at a safe distance in expectation of his friend's coming reaction. It didn't take long.

"Wait, I think I may have misheard you. Did you say 'mates'?"

"Yeah, I did."

"You over-ambitious, sex-crazed, sly little sonofabitch! How the hell did you pull that off? It's a good thing you're gay and can't get them with child. They are men, right?"

Seth laughed. "Yes, they're men. I don't think Fate would be that cruel. Well, strike that, she might be, just not about the parts of their anatomy."

"Oh no. What has the bitch got into this time?"

Aquene's love-hate relationship with their Gods never ceased to amaze him. "I was willing to forgive her the mistake of trying to keep me from meeting my first mate, but she knew I had a second out there and refused me knowledge of him as well." His confession was greeted by silence on the other end, but he knew he had Aquene's undivided attention.

"Aquene, when I confronted her about it, she alluded to the possibility that my second mate's life could be in danger. She said he was supposed to have died before I ever got the chance to meet him, but she acted as though she was unaware that he still lived. I've never known Fate lose track of the death of a mate."

More silence followed, then finally, "Is he safe now? Do you have them both with you?"

"Not in my house. I've been dating Loland for a while now. He's human and I wanted to ease him into the knowledge of our existence. He told me he had an open relationship with his boyfriend. I thought I could get around that, but his lover turned out to be my second mate, which I just discovered earlier tonight after meeting him for the first time."

"That's good, right? If your mates are already intimate with each other, it should ease the way for you."

"It should, but Aquene…Jamie, my second mate, is a Keeper. One who was apparently raised by humans and whom Fate has been unable to keep track of."

The silence this time was so profound that a sense of foreboding settled uneasily into the pit of Seth's stomach.

"Aquene?" No reply. After a few minutes, he checked his cell phone to make sure they hadn't been disconnected. "Friend, I need your help in this. Do you know something I should be aware of?"

"Yes. No, maybe. Fuck! I can't give you any answers right now. Let me do a little research and poking around, find out what I can. Meanwhile, I need you to send me all of the information you can find on your second mate. I assume since you barely met him you'll be trying to learn a lot more about him?"

"Of course."

"Good. Keep me posted periodically. Oh, and Seth?"

"Yeah?"

"Move him in with you immediately. Both men. I don't think your human is in danger, but do not let your Keeper out of your sight, you hear me? Do not let him communicate with any of the Gods, and don't let him outside on his own. In fact, hang up this phone right now and collect them."

"You want me to go over to their house right now and force them to move in with me?"

"Yes."

The conviction and finality in Aquene's voice brooked no argument. The man was half a millennium his senior, which was why Seth deferred to his wisdom whenever in doubt, but there was definitely something going on here that his friend was refusing to clue him in on.

"Aquene, you're scaring me."

"Right back at ya, man, but you're going to have to trust me on this. Leave. Now. Send me an email as soon as you get back. Name, past, former locations. I need everything you can get on Jamie."

Seth could feel his anger building again at the complication his life had suddenly become. The addition of Jamie was a blessing and an enigma all at once. "All right, but let me know as soon as you hear anything. If I'm going to keep him safe, I need to know exactly what, or who, I'm up against."

"Let's just hope it's not the Gods themselves." With that, his friend hung up and he was left staring at his cell phone, trying like hell not to bash it against the wall in frustration. If he had to deal with one more vague comment before this night finally ended, he wouldn't be held accountable for his actions.

Chapter Four

Thirty minutes later, he pulled up at the small house containing his mates and mentally debated the wisdom of what he was about to do. It would be a rude awakening, to say the least, and he prayed to every God he worshipped that the men would still speak to him after this. Hopefully the rapport he'd built so far with Loland would stand him in good stead.

Time to wake up his boys.

He didn't hear any sounds until the third time he knocked on the front door. Then there was a low curse followed by the clinking of metal as locks were unbolted. He'd been surprised by the amount of security upon his earlier visit, but now it seemed insufficient in light of the danger Jamie potentially faced.

A crown of mussed curls peeked around the chain still latched to the door, until Seth could make out Loland's sleepy brown eyes. "Sir? What are you doing...I mean, is something wrong?"

Seth smiled at his catch. It went a long way in demonstrating his trust that Loland remembered to talk with respect to his Dom, who had shown up like a stalker at his house in the middle of the night. "No, nothing is wrong. Not yet, at least. Can I come in and talk with you?"

"Of course."

Seth waited patiently for Loland to remove the chain and bar of steel he knew was wedged between the door and the wall on the floor. He slipped inside and made sure to secure the door again before trailing the sexy man dressed only in loosely-fitting, cotton boxers to the kitchen.

It took only two seconds to decide that once Jamie felt comfortable in their new home, his first rule would be that his boys remain naked at all times while inside. Getting Jamie to submit to him would take some work, but he didn't think it was anything he couldn't handle.

His cock jerked at the memory of the fey features and slim figure of the man sleeping in the other room. He was gorgeous, but the haunted, dull look Seth had glimpsed in his eyes was more than troubling.

"Coffee?"

"Yes, please. I'm sorry to wake you so early, but I need to discuss some things with you."

Loland nodded his head while he busied himself with the coffee maker. Seth knew he was still half-asleep, so he chose an eye-opener as his first question. "Loland, tell me about Jamie's power."

That more than did the job. Loland swung around so quickly that the grounds in the scoop he was holding flew across the floor in a wide arc. His eyes were huge and he opened and closed his mouth several times before he managed to find his voice.

"How do you know?"

Seth calmly walked over to a sprawling ivy plant hanging from the ceiling in a corner beside the fridge and said, "Because I imagine he can do something a little like this." He focussed a small amount of the energy he'd already absorbed from Loland into his fingertips and gently transferred it to the plant. Within seconds, its leaves perked up with vitality and new buds began to form along its delicate vines.

He wasn't quite sure what he'd expected Loland's reaction to be, but it definitely wasn't the response he got. After his boy recovered from his initial shock, he walked slowly forwards and knelt at Seth's feet, keeping eye contact the entire time. Loland then wrapped his arms around Seth's legs and leaned his head into his groin. It wasn't meant to be sexual, and for once Seth's cock obeyed him and remained at half-mast.

"You're like him, aren't you? Thank you, thank you. You have no idea what this means. For years I've been the only one he could confide in, but I have no idea how to help him."

The words were heartfelt and Seth reached down to gather his lover in his arms when he saw tears sparkling on Loland's lashes. He couldn't imagine the confusion and isolation Jamie's gift must have caused both men without proper tutoring, but he could at least do something about it now.

"Take a seat, boy. I'll finish the coffee." He guided Loland to the table and sat him down in one of the high-backed chairs. He found a broom in the narrow utility closet off to the side and began sweeping up the mess on the floor. "Why don't you tell more about Jamie? You've spoken of your current relationship with him, but I need to know of his past, how you came to meet him."

There was still some reservation in Loland's face, which was understandable considering the circumstances, but Seth couldn't afford to lose his faith now. "Tell you what, if you tell me as much as you feel comfortable with now, I'll let you know how it is that I have the same power as Jamie."

That seemed to ease the man's worries a degree. Seth leant back against the counter while the coffee started to brew.

"I met him at...at a mental hospital."

Okay, not the start he had envisioned but interesting nonetheless. Seth worked to keep his expression neutral as he asked, "Why were you in a mental institute?"

A burst of disgust and exasperation left Loland's lips. "I was a regular teenager running around, succumbing to peer pressure and getting into more trouble than I could handle. Nothing really serious. Shoplifting here, cheating on tests there. Then one day, I got the wonderful idea to tell my parents that I was gay. I guess that was the last straw. The next morning, my bags were packed and they shipped me off to Three Parks Mental Health Facility. After their insurance ran out, they convinced the state to take over the funding to keep me in there."

"Baby, I'm so sorry. That must have been rough."

Loland shook his head as if to brush off the memories. "Yeah, it was, but it was nothing compared to what Jamie went through. I think taking care of him saved me from dwelling on my own problems."

A crease furrowed his mate's brow and he paused for several minutes. Seth used this time to pour their coffee and take a seat across from the man at the table. He wanted to prompt Loland to continue, but he also dreaded hearing what he was sure would be even more disturbing revelations.

When Loland met his gaze again, there were fresh tears coating his lashes. "Jamie was twelve when he was admitted. I met him three years after that. I didn't see the signs at first. I was young and naïve. I'd never been exposed to abuse before. It belonged in a world outside of my own. Beyond my comprehension. And he was so drugged up all the time that when he wasn't locked in the isolation tank or strapped to his bed, he looked like he was suffering from severe autism. It was easy to believe that his diagnosis of schizophrenia was true."

Loland drew in a quivering breath and gripped his mug with such force that his knuckles turned white. "One night, I heard someone crying and went to investigate. I found Jamie in his room, bound to the rails of his bed, but completely lucid. There was blood on his sheets. Blood in his mouth.

"I wanted to get help, to let somebody know that he was hurt, but he talked me out of it. He refused to reveal the man who was abusing him, but I did everything I could after that to look out for him. I would visit him at night when his door wasn't locked and became his shadow during the day. He hated it at first."

Loland let out a brief, nostalgic laugh. "He was every bit as stubborn and pig-headed as he is now, but he eventually trusted me with his secrets. He showed me the same trick you pulled off just now with the plant. Said he could also feel the energy of the people around him. I didn't fully understand what he meant at the time, but I knew he was different. Believing in him made more sense to me than anything I had learned that whole year I'd spent at the institute."

"What happened after that?"

"I was released when I turned eighteen. I had an uncle who was an attorney and still speaking to me back then, and I convinced him to help me gain guardianship of Jamie so he could be released into my custody. It took me six months to find a job and push the paperwork through, but at least I knew that Jamie was safe during that time."

"His abuser was no longer working there when you got out?"

"By the time I left, I'd found out who he was despite Jamie's reluctance to tell me. Within twenty-four hours, the guy was admitted to the trauma ward in a hospital and after a three-week vacation there, he decided to terminate his employment. You didn't honestly think I'd let my baby suffer if I could help it now, did you Sir?"

Seth threw his head back and laughed as loudly as he dared, not wanting to wake up the subject of their conversation just yet. The pride he felt for his mate swelled in his chest as the tension in the room gave way to Loland's own levity.

"Not for a moment. I guess that leaves me with just one more question." He hated to kill their brief respite from drama, but the subject had to be addressed before he could pursue both mates without risking either relationship. Since time was of the essence, he figured the blunt approach would be the best. Gods help him.

"Loland, I know we've talked about what it would mean if I became your Master, but I can't do that without including Jamie. I want him to be a part of us. I want to be able to collar you both. How do you feel about that?"

The lust and enthusiasm in Loland's eyes was plain to see, but to his credit, he took the time to mull over this new prospect before giving his answer. If he'd agreed immediately, Seth might have doubted the man's willingness to take Jamie's welfare into full consideration.

The variable of past abuse was nothing to take lightly, and from what he understood, Jamie was not into the lifestyle as much as Loland was, but he hoped there would be room for changes. Well, *more* changes. He had yet to tackle the feat of convincing both men to move in with him without having to resort to physical measures.

"Jamie knows all about the lifestyle, which is why he's fine with my searching for the right Dom. He knows what I need and in a way, I am *his* Dom, but at the same time, I don't think I give him everything that he needs. I can see that he loses touch with reality at times. He's withdrawn from society, but I can't force him to go out into public with his powers. I think that, maybe, he could improve if given the right form of guidance.

"He submits to me but I'm not a Dom, I'm simply the only lover he's ever known. He's never really got the chance to experience anything else. If you'd be willing, I'd love to introduce him to new things with you. I trust you to do that. We haven't known each other for too long, but I do. Is that wrong?"

"No, it's not wrong. There is a reason why we met, which I'll explain to you later, but I'm honoured to know that you have such trust in me. I would never force you or Jamie into a situation either of you were uncomfortable with. I hope you know that."

Seth instantly regretted his words. The whole purpose of this visit was to persuade them to move into his home. He cringed at the thought of what he had to do next, but his thoughts were cut off by a gut-wrenching cry from the other side of the house.

"Shit!" Loland jumped up and bounded out of the room with Seth close on his heels. His mate threw open the door to his bedroom but stopped so suddenly that Seth had to catch him to keep them both from falling forwards from the collision.

The tiny form of his other mate writhed on the bed, obviously caught in the throes of a nightmare. Sweat poured from his pale skin and pooled in the sheets that were wrapped so tightly around him, they restricted his movements. Hushed, mewling noises escaped his lips as he thrashed wildly about. Lines of pure fear creased his face until Seth couldn't take it anymore. His need to comfort his mate was overwhelming.

Just as he was about to rush forwards, Loland placed a firm hand in the centre of his chest and shook his head vehemently. He wanted to disregard the man's warning in the face of Jamie's pain, but he had to trust Loland's experience in this area. The thought of inadvertently causing his little Keeper harm due to his negligence was one he couldn't live with.

Loland crept silently over to the edge of the bed and made shushing noises while rubbing the palm of his hand in a circular motion on Jamie's abdomen. Seth noted the fact that Loland didn't bother to secure the smaller man's arms. Instead, he stayed out of reach of his fists until Jamie eventually began to calm under his lover's gentle ministrations. This was a ritual, Seth realised. One that he suspected happened more often than not.

"What is it, baby?"

At first, Seth thought Loland was addressing him, but to his surprise, Jamie blinked open his sky-blue eyes and responded as though he'd been fully aware of his surroundings the entire time.

"He's coming. Lo, he's coming. He knows where I am now. You have to get away. It's me that he wants."

Loland let out a tired sigh as if he'd heard those lines a thousand times before. "No one is coming after you, Jamie. You're not in any danger and I won't let anyone else hurt you again. Can't you understand that? I'll always protect you, and Seth is going to help." Loland turned a beseeching gaze on him, pleading with his eyes to confirm that everything would be okay, but Seth couldn't make that promise.

"Loland, has someone already tried to make an attempt on his life?"

Loland scowled and said, "Of course not. He was badly beaten by a man I refused as a Master, but I don't think the asshole was out to kill him. Besides, he's in jail now on some other charge — forgery or something like that. Jamie just has nightmares. Nothing serious."

Seth felt like his head was going to explode with all of the information he kept being given that only produced more questions instead of answers. Even if the perp Loland was speaking of wasn't involved in the mysterious scheme against Jamie, the chill warning of his mate's words were too much of a coincidence to ignore.

He would find out later how Jamie was aware that his life was in danger while Loland was still apparently ignorant, but for now, all that mattered was getting them out of here. He intoned, in his most domineering voice, "Get dressed, both of you. Pack one bag with whatever you absolutely need for the night and meet me at the front door in ten minutes."

Jamie jerked his head around Loland's body, his shocked gaze just now registering Seth's presence.

"Sir, he has these nightmares all the time. Almost every night lately, but I don't think we need to..."

"Boy, I'm asking you to trust me when I say that the intricacies of the power Jamie and I possess extend well beyond your current knowledge. I believe there may be more to his dreams than we know of. I would just feel a lot better if I had the two of you under my roof where I can provide additional protection if needed. Temporarily, of course."

He could see the grim acceptance of his reasoning on Loland's face, but before he could respond, Jamie exploded from the bed in a fury.

Jamie felt a wave of betrayal barrel through his chest. He looked to Loland to see the apologetic confirmation in his eyes. The man knew of his powers. His lover had told Seth about his secrets.

Without his knowledge. Without his permission. Memories of drugs and pain consumed him until he couldn't think, couldn't hear past the accusations of insanity.

They would come to take him away and lock him up for good this time. Ironically, the lyrics of the song, *"They're coming to take me away, ha ha,"* rang through his mind as a chasm of despair opened up before him, threatening to swallow him whole if he didn't escape.

Hands and legs tried to slow him down but he twisted away. Once his feet were under him, he raced for the only source of light he could find, intent upon taking whatever measures necessary to gain his freedom.

Steel bands clamped his arms to his sides and he was crushed face-first into a warm, unyielding wall. His head was pressed firmly into a soft crevice, forcing him to concentrate on his breathing, but at this point, he was willing to sacrifice survival if it meant never having to return to that hell.

He renewed his struggles, but within the span of a heartbeat, the frantic adrenaline he'd been using to push himself beyond his limits dissolved in a rush. He was left cold, trembling, and at the mercy of the man holding him. His legs were swept out from under him and folded up against the same slab of muscle the rest of his body was compressed to. Rational thought made a fleeting appearance, though it only served to make him believe he truly was going insane.

Did they make chests this big? He was sure that's what he was being squashed against, but really, this was ridiculous. He didn't think he was that small. Every inch of his skin tingled at the tight embrace he was helpless to break, as though he were enfolded in a blanket of flesh. Warm flesh. Strong, unyielding flesh that beat out the rhythm of a steady, reassuring heartbeat.

Then came the vibrations. They rumbled from the man into his very bones like a soothing melody that never ended. His will to resist the calming effect of that deep resonance bled away like the wisps of a rolling fog under the brilliance of the early morning sun.

It was peaceful here. A place of solace in the midst of his worst nightmare. Eventually, the lull of the beautiful voice speaking in relaxing tones and the incredible warmth that surrounded him became too much to resist, and he slipped mercifully into a dreamless sleep.

* * * *

Jamie awoke to the most wonderful beat thumping through his skull. It was strong, yet leisurely. As though nothing in the world could force it to adapt to anything other than the serenity it tapped out. Steady and sure.

His skin felt ablaze with heat both beneath him and above. It was stifling but reassuring, and when he tried to move, two sets of arms tightened around him, holding him in place. He should have felt the fear that always consumed him when he was unable to move, but it never came. When he turned his head short hairs tickled his nose but the scent that he inhaled was more than worth the nuisance.

Musk, dark spices and a hint of Loland combined to make a heady fragrance that he couldn't seem to get enough of. He rubbed his face in the bristles, trying to soak up more of the intoxicating aroma. A soft rumble of laughter echoed through his front then another slid along his spine. One he was more than familiar with, but the other...Jamie snapped open his eyes to meet a clear, silver gaze. In it, he saw tenderness and patience in a face that was as handsome as it was frightening. There was no masking the raw power behind those sharp angles and planes.

Jamie attempted to scoot away with a start but the body lying against his back only pressed closer, effectively trapping him. He was able to twist his neck just enough to make out copper curls gleaming in the muted light streaming in through a window.

The presence of his lover soothed his nerves a little but he was still embarrassed to find himself made the meat in a sandwich of flesh. Okay, that was the wrong image. His prick began to swell and he desperately attempted to swivel his hips to hide his arousal but there was no room. He was trapped. Alarm set in and memories of last night flooded his mind, bringing with them the sharp sting of Loland's broken promise.

"I can't do this. Let me out. Get off!" He wriggled and shoved at limbs and chests until he'd worked his way free, pulling half of the covers with him and off Loland. The shock of the cold, wooden floor on his bare feet made him forget his anger long enough to take in the appearance of the two men sprawled on the bed.

Loland was completely naked while Seth lay on top of the covers in nothing but silk pyjama bottoms. They were both sweaty and gorgeous. Firm and defined. A smattering of short, black hairs covered Seth's chest and trailed down past the waistband of his pants. Had Jamie been lying on top of him?

The sight took his breath away, causing temporary amnesia, and he struggled to remember why on earth he had wanted to escape such succulent temptation.

Then Seth sat up, breaking his trance. A quick study of his surroundings showed foreign territory. The comfort of familiar furniture had been replaced with pieces that looked antique and well above the price budget of his and Loland's income. The stability he'd built with his lover was floundering and his place in the world was once more being brought into stark question.

A glance down at his body showed his own nakedness and his hands automatically reached to cover the jagged scars across his chest and abdomen. The majority of them were on his backside and the backs of his thighs, so he was relatively safe from scrutiny so long as he didn't turn around. But it was yet another betrayal.

He'd only ever allowed Loland to see his disfigurement. Most times, even with Loland, he kept himself covered or made sure they made love in the dark. Yet here he was, forced to bear his shame in front of two flawless specimens of men. Tears gathered in his eyes but he blinked them back.

"Jamie." The lash of Seth's voice was deep and commanding, but not harsh. "Loland didn't tell me anything about your power that I hadn't already realised upon meeting you last night. I have that same power and it's nothing to be ashamed of. I'd like to teach you about our history, if you're willing. I asked Loland to come to my house with you because it would be easier this way for me to train you.

"You see, you're not alone in this. There are thousands more like us. I won't push you into learning if you're not ready, but please consider staying here at least until Loland returns from his trip. I wouldn't feel right leaving you on your own."

Seth had him until that last part. Jamie growled at the implied reference to his weakness. "I can take care of myself."

"Oh, I know. I never doubted that."

That response brought Jamie up short, cutting off his next retort. He defiantly met Seth's stare, searching for any trace of mockery or deceit, but finding none.

"There's also another reason why I wanted to lure you here, but I think I'll let my boy explain that one." Seth casually leaned over and claimed Loland's mouth in a possessive kiss. Jamie watched as his lover melted into the larger man in much the same way Jamie melted into Loland when they kissed.

Seth wrapped his arm around Loland's waist and pulled him close so that their hips met, trapping Loland's straining erection between his thighs. Soft moans erupted from Loland's lips and were swallowed by Seth's greedy mouth as they ground their cocks against each other in a seductive play of dominance and submission.

An unbidden vision of himself lying between them, swaying back into Loland only to be thrust into Seth's strong embrace invaded his mind. It had nothing to do with his precog and everything to do with the sexual desire racing through his veins at the erotic sight before him.

His hand found his cock without thought and stroked it in long, yearning pulls. A small groan slipped past his control and he blushed furiously when he saw Seth turn his gaze on him. He stopped pumping himself but his stubborn hand remained secured to his prick in a tight grip. To his utter humiliation, he whimpered when Seth released Loland and walked to the bedroom door.

"I expect you both down for breakfast in no more than thirty minutes." The huge man closed the door behind him, leaving Jamie to face his slightly amused lover.

"Admit it. You want him."

"No," Jamie denied. "I only want you. I can't... Lo, what's going on here?"

Loland rolled over and slid off the edge of the bed, walking towards him in that sexy, alluring stride that always made his mouth water in anticipation. Sure hands found their way around his lean hips, pulling him in to the fold of Loland's warm body.

"I love you, you know that, but we both know that you crave the same thing I do. The ability to surrender without pain. Please don't worry that I'll let you go. That's never going to happen, but this man...I trust him, and he can help you. Not just with your powers, but with other things as well." Loland gazed down into Jamie's wide-eyed stare and feathered his thumb over and over across his cheek as he continued to speak.

"I want him to be my Master. You know what that means, but the only way I will accept him is if he accepts you...and the only way he will accept me is if you can accept him as well. We're a package deal, and Seth understands that like no one I've ever met before. We both want you to be right there with us."

The sincerity in Loland's face was impossible to disclaim, and the buried hunger that his words brought to the surface in Jamie was equally undeniable. Guilt swirled inside of him for keeping a secret from his lover that Loland had known all along. Jamie did long for the same kind of relinquishing of control his lover spoke of desiring.

The contentment of giving oneself over to the dominion of a Master that Loland had described to him time and again had seemed like an unattainable dream that Jamie had never dared to tell Loland of. He'd always feared that Loland would be offended if he knew Jamie desired the kind of dominance that Loland couldn't provide for him.

He wanted so much to believe in Loland's words. Jamie's gaze strayed down the length of Loland's perfect build—free of scars and pain, and filled with muscle mass that Jamie could never hope to build. He didn't bother to compare it to his own damaged body. A choked sob scratched his throat as he realised that Seth must have seen his scars. Testament to his weakness.

Loland must have read his thoughts because the man grabbed him up in a vicious hold and said, "Don't you dare start that. You're beautiful. If you don't believe me, then believe your own eyes. Did Seth indicate in any way that he was disgusted by you?"

Jamie thought hard, wanting to prove Loland wrong if only to justify his self-loathing, but there had been nothing. Nothing except for the intensity of lust, concern, and something he didn't even want to try to identify at this time. He reluctantly shook his head.

Loland pulled back and looked him directly in the eye, demanding his complete attention. "You will always come first in my heart. You know that, right?"

Jamie nodded without hesitation.

"Good. I have two weeks left with the both of you before I have to leave for my business trip. Seth thinks it would be best if you stayed here with him, but neither one of us will force you to it. I want to… *We* want to show you what it can be like. Having a Master. I think that Seth is the one, for both of us, but only if you agree. I want you to get to know him, see if maybe you could like him as much as I do. Will you give him a chance?"

The longing in Loland's eyes was pure. Untainted by the fears of Jamie's own past. And even though the idea of giving his trust to another was anathema from his perspective, he couldn't deny that the prospect of Loland's suggestion was thrilling. He found himself nodding his agreement despite the challenge of the unknown. The brilliant smile that lit up his lover's face at his answer was almost enough to erase his apprehension.

"Thank you. Thank you, baby. I know this isn't easy for you, but we'll take it slow. I promise to give you as much time as you need." Loland grabbed his hand and pulled him towards the adjoining master bathroom.

Chapter Five

During their shower together, Loland skimmed over the basics of the behaviour he would be showing as Seth's submissive, both in and out of his presence. The information was nothing new to Jamie, but he didn't bother to tell Loland of the extensive research he had done out of personal curiosity and hidden desire.

The more Loland described the domestic role he was about to undertake with Seth, the harder Jamie's cock grew. Thankfully, Loland only acknowledged his arousal with an understanding grin.

Once they were dressed, they headed down a winding staircase and followed the delicious smells of coffee and eggs past a voluminous foyer and into a kitchen that was more than double the size of their living room. He wanted to feel disdain for Seth's extravagant display of wealth in owning such a large house with only himself to occupy it, but he tempered his reaction as the things that were missing caught his eye.

The walls were vaulted and white, but bare of any personal photos or memorabilia. Sparse pieces of austere furniture held nothing more significant than detached adornments obviously hand-picked by a sophisticated yet impersonal decorator. Design might be his partner's domain, but even he could see that there was no love or happiness displayed within the ensemble of this house.

"You know how you're always telling me that a man's home reflects his heart?" Jamie asked.

"Just as I always tell you that what's not in his home can reflect the love that he's missing?"

Touché.

The kitchen continued the same aloofness with its severely patterned black-and-white tiled floor and coordinating appliances. Jamie had grown up around people who had drooled and dreamt about owning such opulent houses like this. For him, however, the only endearing feature he could find was the tall man leaning over the oven, burning his hand on a baking pan filled with golden biscuits.

The energy in his body reacted to Seth's presence like wildfire. It blazed through him, causing his breath to quicken and his cock to fill until it was as hard as nails. What *was* it about this man that had him reacting in a way only Loland had inspired in him before?

Loland led him to a breakfast nook in the corner which contrasted with the modern appliances inhabiting the rest of the room. The wooden booths were comfortably padded in bright colours and a soft blue cloth covering the table was outfitted with three placement settings in colours just as cheery.

Jamie was sure that Seth was aware of their presence, but he gave no indication as he continued with his cooking. Or self-mutilation, depending on how one looked at it.

The booths were placed in an L-shape with a separate bench lining the third side of the table. Jamie slid into a booth, expecting Loland to join him, but he was surprised when his lover simply leant down and whispered in his ear, "Remember baby, I love you. If you decide you want to leave or join us or ask a question, just let us know. Seth wants to get to know you, so don't be afraid to communicate your needs."

Jamie didn't quite understand his words until Loland straightened and joined Seth, only he didn't offer any help. Loland stood to the side with his back straight, legs slightly apart, and hands folded behind his back. His head was held high but his lashes fanned his cheeks as he kept his gaze on the floor.

It was a position, Jamie realised. He'd seen many postures of submission in the research on BDSM he'd conducted on the Internet, but this was the first time he had seen someone actually assume one.

At first, he was angered that Seth continued to ignore Loland as the man piled food onto plates and poured coffee, but the growing excitement he could feel radiating from Loland told him that he was enjoying himself. When the last of the ingredients had been put away, Seth finally turned to Loland and gave him a critical once-over, then turned his full attention to Jamie.

His silver eyes softened as he said, "I assume that Loland has explained to you that I hope we can get to know each other better, and that you've agreed to see where this leads by the fact that you're still here."

Jamie wanted the assurance of Loland's confident presence by his side, but something in the tone Seth used with him offered its own semblance of succour to his rattled nerves. "Yes, Sir."

"Good. I want to reiterate what Loland said earlier and make sure you know that if at any time you feel uncomfortable with what we're doing or with staying here, we will listen and adjust our plans accordingly."

That sounded a little vague compared to the words Loland had used, but again, his anxiety was placated by the man's forwardness. "Yes, Sir."

Seth seemed to be satisfied with his answer. He turned back to Loland's silent form and developed that same commanding tone that Jamie was beginning to recognise as his serious voice. "Do you need to go into work today, boy?"

"No, Sir. I do need to call my boss and confirm the flight reservations by noon, but my research for the design of the hotel can be conducted over the Internet. I need to finish the job that I'm currently working on, but my customer won't be available until next week."

"Good. Strip. While you are here, you will remain naked at all times. If someone knocks on the door, you will report it to me immediately, although I'm not expecting any visitors this weekend. If you get too hot or cold, you are to let me know. I am responsible for your wellbeing, and if I find that you are sacrificing your comfort simply to please me, you will be punished."

By the time Seth stopped talking, Loland had divested himself of all but his underwear, which he was pulling down with haste and folding neatly onto the pile of his clothes he'd stacked on the counter next to him. His cock was stiff and made even more obvious when Loland again assumed his position of servitude.

Seth made a slow circuit around him, adjusting Loland's posture to his specifications. Each touch from Seth sent an electric jolt that Jamie could sense through Loland's body. The procedure seemed calculated and distanced on Seth's part, until Jamie noticed the sizeable bulge in the front of the large man's pants.

The sight of Loland's hard stomach and tanned flesh had Jamie's own cock straining against the seam of his jeans. He lowered his hand to adjust himself but stopped as Seth took notice and gave him a stern look. Unexpected pleasure stole into him at the look of satisfaction Seth sent him when he pulled his hand away without completing his task.

"Take these to the table, boy." He handed Loland two plates full of food then reached to carry the rest of the breakfast items behind him. Seth sat at the bench but when Loland moved to join Jamie in the booth, Seth grabbed his wrist and guided him to a kneeling position on a soft mat next to his feet. Loland obeyed instantly and tried to hide the smile that curved his lips at Seth's insistence that he stay near.

During the meal, Seth fed Loland and went over the same set of rules for Loland's behaviour that Loland had told him about in the shower. Jamie knew he should keep his guard up against the total sphere of control the man imposed, but he was too caught up in the look on Loland's face. He seemed...at peace.

The rules mainly involved behaviour that reinforced Seth's role as Master and Loland's role as sub. Seth also went over his and Loland's hard boundaries and gave examples of a few of the rewards he would dole out for good behaviour.

Most of it Jamie had already heard from Loland. His lover had stayed up with him many nights, even before meeting Seth, describing his likes and dislikes, his dreams and hopes. But the way that Seth's gaze fixed on Jamie as often as on Loland during the entire speech made all of the information seem new and intense. It was as though Seth were measuring Jamie's reactions to his words. What he found there, Jamie had no clue, but a small smile played on the man's lips as he finished the last of his eggs.

"Jamie, I understand that this is all fairly new to you, but I'd like to know how open you are to the idea of letting me dominate you. We would need to build up to a level of trust that both you and I are comfortable with, but I'd like to start our relationship in a Dom/sub context. I don't want to assume that because it works for me and Loland, it will work for you as well."

Jamie's cock thickened even more at the picture the man's words painted. He could see why Loland had fallen in love with him. Seth was extraordinarily handsome and seemed like the kind of man who was willing to take the time to nurture a meaningful relationship instead of just a quick fuck. Jamie suspected that Loland knew of his desire for more domination than Loland could provide, but what if he didn't meet Seth's standards?

Jamie looked to Loland for reassurance. He had absolute faith in him, and Loland obviously felt secure in the promises Seth offered.

Yet he still felt lost.

Loland read in his expression what he couldn't say aloud. "Sir, Jamie wants to say that he would like you to dominate him, but he needs some time to adjust."

Jamie nodded his head vigorously, ashamed that his partner had to relate his wishes, but grateful as well. Seth deliberated for a minute then finally nodded. What the man thought of his cowardice, Jamie couldn't tell, but he felt relief at the grin on Loland's face.

"We'll start with simple things, then. Tonight we'll create schedules for both of you. After that, Jamie, we'll make a list of commands you can handle right now and go from there. Meanwhile, Loland can show you where I've already set up your computer and fax machine in my office for your work. You can write down anything else you think you'll need here while he makes his phone calls. Other than that, the day is yours. Any room in the house is open to you, and the grounds are extensive and bordered by a large privacy fence that runs along the perimeter."

Seth gave Loland a soft kiss on his forehead. "I want you both back here by noon for lunch. Take your cell phone with you while you're roaming around, that way you can call me if you need anything or have a question."

"Sir?"

Jamie knew exactly what Loland was going to ask. He heard it every time Loland came back from the grocery store with new recipes in hand. A giggle escaped before he clapped his hand over his mouth and met Seth's curious gaze.

"What is it, boy?"

"Can I...with your permission, make lunch, and dinner maybe? Not that your cooking isn't good, but I found a new recipe last week that I noticed you had all of the ingredients for and wanted to try it."

Seth arched an eyebrow. "I see you've been making yourself at home already."

Loland ducked his head. "Only in the kitchen so far, Sir. I'm sorry, but I couldn't help myself. Food is a form of decoration. It calls to me."

"Don't ever apologise for wanting to do something that comes naturally to you. Nothing in my home or on my lands is off limits to either of you...except for the playroom in the basement, but only because I want that to be a surprise. We'll wait until you're both ready to explore it. Call me when you have lunch prepared." Seth stood and walked over to Jamie, surprising him with a small kiss on the crown of his head before leaving the room.

The sigh from Loland echoed Jamie's thoughts, but he wasn't about to admit the strong reaction he was having to Seth's dominance until he was certain Loland was okay with it.

"Come on, baby. Help me clean up here so we can explore this place. It's just screaming at me to be pampered and adored. It may look barren, but the shape of the walls and the layout are optimum for maximum exposure.

"This house was built to inspire the kind of welcoming charm I've always dreamt of creating in a home. Can you imagine if we were to live here? I just know that Seth would thrive under the kinds of changes I have in store. With your green thumb, you could transform every empty room into a living, colourful entity. It would be wonderful, don't you think?"

"Does that mean you want to move in here?" There was no hiding the trepidation in his voice. Things were happening so fast that he was having a hard time wrapping his mind around the changes. He wanted so much to please but was afraid of failure.

"Oh sweetheart, I'll never leave you behind." Loland faced him but creased his brow as if searching for the right words to explain how he felt.

"You love him."

It wasn't a question, and it wasn't denied. "I think I might. I'm not sure yet. I've only ever loved you, and I knew that first moment I saw you. I think I want to love him, but he said something last night that I realised would be, *should* be true, no matter what happens in my life."

Jamie barely managed to swallow past the lump forming in his throat. "What was that?"

"He said that he and I could never have a true relationship unless you were a part of it. I could never love a man who didn't love you as much as I do. He told me he wanted both of us. All of us. Not just me. He made me realise that nothing I find with him would ever be complete unless you were a part of it."

The lump grew to the size of a tennis ball and tears stung his eyes but he refused to give in to the weakness of his emotions. "He said that?"

Loland walked up to him and cradled his face gently in his hands. "Yes, he did. All we're asking of you is a chance, but you are and always will be my first priority. Say the word and we'll leave. Or stay. I want you to be happy."

Just like that. The simplicity of Loland's words and the earnestness in his eyes showed him a world without the fear that he constantly lived with despite his lover's diligent protection of him. Could it really be that easy? Could he learn to love the bear Loland was obviously smitten with? Maybe. At that moment, everything inside him wanted to try to attain that level of harmony, but what if the bear couldn't love him as he did Loland?

"I love you, Lo. I trust you. And I...I think I do want him to dominate me. Everything about him scares me, but I can feel what you see in him, and I'm tired of being afraid all the time. I don't think he would hurt me like...like that man at the hospital, but I want to feel the pleasure in the pain that you told me he gives you. Is that okay?"

"Of course, baby. I'm so proud of you, but you have to promise me that you won't ever make any decisions based on what you think will please me. The glory of submission can be found in the service of someone you care about, but your own needs should always come first."

"I promise."

"You amaze me. How about we ask Sir to go over your boundaries tonight and our schedules tomorrow, that way we all know where we stand?"

"Can I still call you Sir, too?"

Loland chuckled. "If that's what you want, it's fine by me, but we'll have to come up with some sort of distinction between me and Seth."

Jamie nodded and sighed. Maybe it really was as simple as that.

* * * *

An exploration of the rest of the house had proven each room to be as devoid of personal effects as the ones they'd already visited. All except for the study, which struck Jamie as the wrong title for the room he walked into. It was more like a library, with bookcases that lined three of the four walls from floor to ceiling. The fourth wall opposite the door, a good thirty yards away, was filled with original paintings that depicted scenes from every century dating back as far as 600 A.D.

A solid oak, hand-crafted desk easily the size of Loland's Camry stood in front of the wall with a black leather chair pushed into it. Another desk of similar design yet smaller in size resided in front and to the side of it.

On its surface were Jamie's desktop computer and fax machine, as well as several empty office supply containers waiting to be filled and a landline phone. A soft brown leather chair sat at that desk, turned towards the door as if to invite its owner to make use of it. Multiple hand-sewn rugs were strewn about the room, adding an array of colours to the more sedate furnishings and panelled walls.

Loland kept him company while he discovered the wonders of the books that swept him away into other worlds as he delved into their stores of knowledge. He was reluctantly pulled away from his investigation for lunch and dinner, which were conducted in the same manner as breakfast, only with the familiar flavours of Loland's cooking.

He responded to Seth's enquiries as to how he was enjoying the house, but his answers were limited considering the fact that he'd spent most of his time in the man's study.

Seth didn't seem to mind, though. He suggested books he thought Jamie might be interested in and continued to feed Loland at his feet and praise him for the delicious meal with soft caresses and kind words. Loland soaked it up with every ounce of his being and kept sending excited glances in Jamie's direction.

Watching Loland submit to his attractive Dom — in the buff, with his cock standing at attention and leaking fluid every time Seth grazed his fingers along his smooth skin — was almost too much to bear. More than once, Jamie imagined himself in Loland's position. He envisioned what it must be like to be able to let go of his constant stress, to trust in the care of someone else.

As he watched the pair, he noticed that Seth didn't seem to take pride in what most people did when they spent time with their partner. The admiration Loland received from Seth didn't hinge on his conversational skills or his physical beauty. All it took was his willingness to be attended to by a man who accepted him for who he was.

The demand was there, but even Jamie could see that it was Loland's choice as to whether or not he wanted to meet that demand.

"Jamie? I'd like your perspective on that."

Seth's deep voice pulled him out of his reverie. "Sir?"

"Loland tells me that you would like to go over the boundaries of your submission tonight, but I need to hear it from you. This is not something to be taken lightly, but we can take it as slowly as you need it to go."

Was it that time already? Somehow the hours of the day he had planned to use to prepare for this discussion had slipped by him. He wasn't ready. What if he did something wrong? Said something wrong? What if he wasn't able to please Seth as much as Loland pleased him? He didn't know if he could deal with their disappointment in his failure. Then again, how could he live with himself if he passed up the opportunity he'd been dreaming about for years?

"Yes, Sir. If it's all right with you, I want to...submit to you."

The tender smile that softened Seth's lips caused his stomach to flutter in anticipation. "Good boy. Let's adjourn to the living room. Leave the dishes until we're done with our discussion."

Jamie and Loland followed him into the living room and sat side by side on the couch as directed. Seth pulled aside the coffee table in front of them and replaced it with the recliner so that he sat directly in front of them.

"First of all, I want to say that nothing that is suggested by any of us will become a rule until we all agree to it. Consider this a democratic meeting. But once the rules are settled and agreed upon by everyone, they fall under my dictatorship. I am trusting that you'll be honest in your needs and boundaries just as you are trusting me to keep you safe...even from myself if I should lose control for any reason. Is this understood?"

Jamie and Loland nodded their heads but when Seth continued to look at them expectantly, they both said, "Yes, Sir."

"You will answer my questions with verbal responses at all times so that there is no confusion. You will never raise your voices to me. Anything worth listening to can be said in a quiet, respectful manner. Now Jamie, am I right to assume that you're aware of Loland's hard limits and would like to establish those same limits in regards to yourself?"

Jamie knew exactly what his lover refused to explore and had always held the same opinion. "Yes, Sir."

"Good. Loland's limits reflect my own so we have no problem there. What are the things you feel you cannot do right now, that you might like to eventually work up to?"

"Nudity." The response was immediate, and one that had been on his mind as he had admired Loland's perfect skin and body throughout the day. He was flawed in more ways than one, and though he knew Seth had already seen his ugliness, he saw no reason to remind the man of it on a constant basis.

"Why?"

Why? Wasn't the answer to that obvious? "I know I'm ugly but..."

"Excuse me?" Seth didn't raise his voice. He didn't need to. The rage was plain to see in his eyes and Jamie flinched at the onslaught of spitting waves of angry energy that rolled off the man. Within seconds it dissipated, but he knew that it wasn't because it no longer existed. The lines on Seth's face told him that the man had merely reined it in instead of letting it go.

"I apologise. I didn't mean to inflict that surge of energy on you, but I can see that I need to address this issue before we go any further. I will not tolerate any allusions to the belief that you are ugly. In fact, I will include something along those lines in your daily routine tomorrow. I understand that you have scars on your body that were placed there against your will, but to assume that either Loland or I find you unattractive is a blatant disregard for our opinion. Do I make myself clear?"

Jamie felt his own anger rise to the surface. "And just what is your opinion, Sir?" he asked in the most sarcastic tone he could muster. How dare the man lie to him? He didn't need anyone's pity or lies. He knew he was ugly. There was no reason for Seth or Loland to ignore the fact.

"You are beautiful. One day you might actually believe me and see for yourself, but until then, you will take my word for it."

Pretty words. He'd heard them all from Loland before but Seth's sexy tone didn't alter the falsehood behind them. "I'm ugly. Can't you see that?" He could hear his voice growing in pitch and volume with each word he spoke, but he was powerless to stop his emotions. "He made me ugly. I know you love Loland but you don't need to lie to me to keep him. You really think seeing the disgust on your faces every day is going to help me?"

The fury that spiked from both men made him instantly regret his words. *Shit shit shit shit shit.* This was a meeting he had asked for to discuss the terms of his submission, yet here he was throwing their good intentions in their faces. Ridiculing them like so many others had ridiculed him in the past.

"I'm sorry. Oh, please, I'm so sorry..."

"Strip."

Seth's demand scattered his thoughts. Somewhere in the back of his mind he realised he was being commanded to do the very thing he had asked to avoid, but he also knew the way he had gone about it was wrong. It was unfair not only to the man who had dedicated his life to making him happy, but also to the man who was willing to risk his relationship with the one he loved just to help him.

Jamie looked to Loland and saw love behind the face of his displeasure. He bowed his head and divested himself of his clothes. His shame beat at him with each rapid pounding of his heart. When he was completely naked, Seth said, "Come here."

By the time he stood in front of Seth, his yearning to beg for forgiveness was almost a tangible entity that clawed at his throat, demanding release. He kept his gaze on Seth's boots and clenched his jaw, afraid that he would only humiliate himself further if he let loosely the storm of remorse building in his mind.

He jerked at the startling touch of Seth's hand on his wrist and allowed the man to pull him down so that he lay across his lap. His hips rested on the tops of his thighs and Seth pushed on the back of his neck until Jamie's head was level with his ankles. His nervousness at being exposed was strangely muted by the reassuring waves of energy rolling off Loland and Seth.

"What did he use to give you these scars?" One of Seth's hands rubbed softly over the length of his back, tracing the proof of his weakness. He hated it. His scars. His inability to defend himself. Seth's kindness. All of it.

"His belt, Sir. His belt and the ropes he tied me down with." His breathing was so erratic by now that he wasn't sure if Seth understood him.

"I'm going to punish you with my hand, Jamie. I'm going to spank you. Your safe word is 'red'. You will use it if you feel that you can't take anymore and once you do, everything will stop. Do you understand why I'm doing this?"

"Y—yes Sir. I disrespected your opinion of me. I'm s—sorry." Even in his misery he felt his cock swell against the side of Seth's thigh. He wanted this. Needed this. Was close to begging for it when the first blow landed with a resounding smack on his left butt cheek. The second followed immediately on his right.

Seth continued at a relentless pace that took his breath away. There was no pause or mercy. The pain quickly became excruciating and he cried out, screamed, begged for it to stop, but Seth only slapped harder. Words poured from his mouth without meaning and tears clogged his eyes and throat. Still the blows landed across his ass, thighs and lower back with increasing vigour.

Time lost all meaning and his world narrowed to the fire in his backside. Memories surged to drown him in images of the past but his mind focussed on the pattern of the blows he was being dealt. Fear existed only in chaos, but the hand that struck him followed a rhythm that centred his riotous emotions.

Just when he thought he would burst from the intensity, the pain suddenly became a part of him, releasing him so that he could take in everything else. The heat scorching his bottom allowed him to concentrate on all that he'd been missing.

The security of Seth's body wrapped underneath and above him. Seth's firm hand at the nape of his neck, anchoring him, promising to keep him safe when he felt as though he would shatter without his support. The care Seth took to calculate each blow so that he could float in the safety he was given without fear of being overwhelmed.

He was caught in a whirlwind of pain and comfort and forgiveness that he never wanted to escape. Here, his ugliness did not exist. This man accepted him, held him, proved that he would never let him go with his firm grip and each forceful strike of his hand.

He could feel pressure building in his groin and more words flowed from his mouth. He knew he was begging, pleading for something, but he wasn't sure what it was that he needed. Fingers surrounded the head of his cock and his hips bucked involuntarily. The cry that vibrated his lips scratched the insides of his throat but he couldn't stop.

He trembled under the force of the blows and the tight pulls on his cock. Hoarse whimpers escaped until he had no choice but to surrender to the demands on his body. His orgasm exploded throughout his entire being, wrenching a scream that he was sure made his throat bleed. He silently begged for Seth to help him through the pleasure as well as thanking him for every deliverance of pain upon his back that eased his emotional release.

When the last of his spasms shot through him, the blows lessened in intensity and he was gradually eased into a cocoon of warmth and safety. Strong arms lifted him and he burrowed into the welcoming embrace.

Chapter Six

Jamie woke up alone the next morning. The sheets on either side of him were cold, confirming he'd been there on his own for quite some time. His mind promptly reviewed the events of the previous evening and he groaned as he realised he had a lot to atone for.

He rolled onto his back to stare at the ceiling while he contemplated his mistakes and rolled right back over onto his belly. Pain blossomed along his ass and thighs, reminding him of the punishment he'd been given.

It had the reverse effect, however. His cock hardened as he recalled the blistering feel of Seth's hand, his unrelenting tone of voice. It had been Loland's touch that had given him the release he'd so desperately needed, but he was sure it had only been at the behest of his Master. Loland's Master...or his? He supposed the only difference lay in the question of whether or not he thought of them as the same man.

Yes. Loland would always be his Sir, but Seth had shown him what a Master could do last night. Jamie didn't think he'd been completely irrational about the reason for his reluctance to remain nude while inside, but he had handled the issue poorly. He'd incited the ire of both his lover and the man he wanted to impress by venting his frustration over his own low self-esteem.

Guilt settled over him like a shroud but he pushed it away. Last night he had lost his temper, but instead of rejecting him, Loland and Seth had taught him a lesson and kept him safe. They deserved a lover who had enough confidence to trust in their opinions.

So far, he wasn't doing so well in that category.

With newfound determination, Jamie left the bed and showered. He wanted to apologise for his behaviour. Thank both men for the best orgasm he'd ever had in his life. Show his appreciation for their patience, but every brush of the washcloth over his bruised skin didn't help matters. His cock throbbed at the memory of being held, cherished. He wanted to return the favour, but he had nothing to give. He was only a submissive.

Jamie chuckled as he realised he'd answered his own question. He was a submissive, and that was all Loland and Seth desired from him. For him to be himself. To give them his submission. He could do that. Not easily, but it was not an impossibility. After stepping out of the shower, he towelled himself dry and gave one last, longing look at the drawer he knew contained his clothes before leaving the room. As he approached the voices he heard from the kitchen, he could feel a knot of anxiety clench around his throat, squeezing until his breathing became laboured. His hands automatically flew to his scars but he forced them back down.

This was his apology. His thanks to them. They had said that they thought him...beautiful...and he had to trust in them. He sucked in a large gulp of air and entered the room.

The silence that followed was deafening and the temptation to run and hide was almost more than he could handle. He couldn't look up or keep from clenching his hands in an effort to hold them at his sides. He couldn't move, so he waited.

"Come here, boy."

The strength in Seth's voice released him and he rushed to the man, but instead of allowing Jamie to kneel beside him, Seth pulled him into his lap and wrapped his powerful arms around him. The breath he'd been holding in rushed from his lungs on a sigh and he leaned in to the embrace.

"Thank you."

Jamie frowned and finally raised his eyes to see Loland beaming at him from his position on the floor and the look of satisfaction on Seth's face above him. "For what?"

"For giving us this—you."

* * * *

The rest of the week was relatively uneventful, much to Jamie's surprise and dismay. He'd managed to complete his list of goals and hard limits without further incident and Seth had worked with both Loland and Jamie to coordinate schedules for them. It was more like a list of chores and obligations, in his opinion, but he wasn't ready to push his luck by complaining just yet.

Maybe next week.

Seth had restricted them from masturbation, fondling, rubbing, groping... He could go on. When Seth had first stated the rule, it had been slightly upsetting, but nothing he couldn't deal with. Then the man had included himself in his edict. They were not allowed to tempt Seth into giving them any sort of sexual gratification…at all.

Jamie was half-tempted to disobey just to feel the pleasure he knew Seth's hand on his backside would bring.

While he could admit that his routine and the forced abstinence allowed him a singular focus that helped him to concentrate more on his submission, it was driving him insane. At the same time, he continued to struggle with his feelings of inadequacy.

Though Seth never displayed a preference between Loland and him, Jamie still could not retain a posture of confidence for long when he assumed his positions for Seth. *Master.* It was the distinction he and Loland had decided on, and surprisingly, it came to him with ease.

"Little one."

Jamie raised his eyes from the untouched plate of food before him and met Seth's unwavering gaze. They were all seated at the breakfast nook for dinner and still dressed from their recent trip to his house to collect more of their things. It felt odd to wear clothes after going for so many days without them, but Seth had demanded that they remain dressed from some reason.

"Yes, Master?"

"I know the past several days haven't been easy for you, but they were meant to be a lesson. Can you tell me what that is?"

Jamie frantically searched his mind for an answer he thought would please the man but could not get past the thoughts that had been plaguing him every minute of every day lately. No sex, rules, no sex, obedience, work, no sex, innocent kisses, no sex…

"I'm sorry, Sir. I don't know."

Seth stood up so abruptly that for a brief moment, Jamie wanted to shout out another apology, but relief flooded through him when Seth said, "If you two would clean up here, I have a surprise for you that I need to make preparations for. Join me in the bedroom when you're done." Seth kissed the crown of first Loland's head then Jamie's before leaving the room. Jamie desperately wanted to ask Loland if he knew what Seth had in mind but bit his tongue.

When the last of the dishes had been put away, Jamie trailed after Loland up the staircase to the master bedroom at the top. He gasped as he took in the interior of the room. The lights were off but rows of candles lit every hard surface along the walls. The effect created a warm glow that softened the rough edges of Seth's features while highlighting his golden skin. He wore nothing but a snug pair of suede pants that matched his short, black hair.

The currents from both Seth and Loland danced along his skin and slid into his body, infusing him with their combined arousal. His breath hitched as he followed the seductive gait of Seth's approach. The man moved like fluid and Jamie decided that the only thing more provocative about him was his voice. The thought drew Jamie's stare to his wide lips and held him immobile.

"Boy, I think our little one still hasn't learned his lesson in appreciation. What do you think?"

"I think you're right, Sir," Loland breathed.

Jamie's eyes widened and his breath quickened, but he couldn't turn away from that intense, silvery gaze. The lust and hunger he saw there was tempered by patience. When Seth had closed the remaining distance between them until their faces were just inches apart, Jamie could feel his calming energy stealing into him with every inhalation.

The other man unhurriedly raised a hand until it cupped his cheek. Though the touch was so soft he could have been imagining it, it burned his skin with delicious heat and before Jamie considered his actions, he leaned in to the embrace.

"I won't hurt you, I promise. I've been watching you appreciate Loland's naked body but I don't think you understand how important it is that you appreciate your own, and let others appreciate your beauty as well."

Jamie opened his lips to let loosely a snort but Seth slid his thumb over to cover them and shook his head slightly.

"I didn't say you could speak." That soft admonishment caused his cock to jerk. "I want you to see what we see when we look at you." Seth's thumb feathered from side to side on his lower lip but those eyes never strayed from his. "If you want us to stop for any reason, you will use your safe word. It will instantly end whatever we're doing without consequences or ridicule. Do you understand?"

Jamie nodded. He remembered the safe word Seth had given him before his punishment. He knew that they were occasionally disregarded by some Doms, resulting in real harm done to the sub. He'd even had personal experience with an overzealous Dom, although in that situation, he'd not been given the option of a safe word.

But this was different. Loland's presence grounded him and Seth's energy was nothing like the suffocating violence of his past attackers.

When Seth continued to stare at him expectantly, he whispered, "Yes, Sir."

"Very good, little one." The large man turned to Loland, still standing at attention. "I want you to undress yourself and then him. Take your time doing it. This need not be rushed." Once Loland had stripped himself of his clothes, Seth removed his hand and stepped away to give Loland room, but his imprint remained like a soothing brand.

Loland replaced Seth's body in front of him. Brown eyes replaced grey, but the energy remained the same. Hands that had explored every curve and hollow on his body hundreds of times in the past skimmed down his neck and over the material of his shirt until they connected with his skin again beneath the hem. They glided up his chest, trailing fire in their wake, until Jamie was forced to raise his arms so his shirt could be removed.

Loland bent his head down to slide his tongue under Jamie's jaw, along his collarbone, then to his nipple. It was caught between teeth and rolled and sucked while every inch of his bare torso was caressed by those magical hands. When he thought he could take no more, his other nipple was dragged into the hot cavern of Loland's mouth, flicked and teased repeatedly. Loland gracefully knelt down and began to work on the buttons of Jamie's jeans, but it suddenly became too much.

Everything was centred on him. His ragged breaths were the only noise that filled the room. Both men silently gauged his reactions and stared at him as if nothing else existed. The attention was more than he was accustomed to and he tried to squirm away but Seth was there with his voice and his words and his tone that brooked no argument.

"Stop concentrating on what you think you should do. No one is here to judge," Seth counselled as Loland pulled down his boxers and jeans, kissing his way down Jamie's legs and licking at sensitive areas. "I want you to give yourself over to the trust you have in Loland." Jamie's brow furrowed. Hadn't he always done that?

As if reading his thoughts, Seth said, "Not like you have in the past. The gift of submission is in the ability to completely surrender yourself to the care of your Master. When you empty your mind and body of everything other than the desire to please him, you are giving him control that is as sexy as it is precious."

His shoes and socks disappeared with his pants but the warmth of Loland's hands and lips was everywhere. Jamie watched him lick and bite every inch he could reach while on his knees and shivered at the visible pleasure his lover found in making sure that no part of him went untouched. Doubt started to cloud the cadence of Seth's voice. The care Loland was taking with him might make him *feel* sexy, but that was a far cry from his actual appearance.

Jamie needed more assurance. He was afraid to speak for fear of saying something wrong, but his concerns were once again dispelled by the rich inflections of Seth's voice.

"The gift of dominance is in the ability to communicate with your partner and discern his needs. A true Master will demand obedience, but he may only do so once he has earned the trust of the submissive. Once he is given control, it is his responsibility to provide for his sub's safety, even if the threat comes from the Master himself."

Jamie was taken aback by that. He broke away from the alluring sight of Loland on his knees and looked to Seth. His heart was beating wildly and his eyes refused to settle on any one feature. Seth was rubbing his cock leisurely through the confines of his pants with one hand while the other was clenched into a tight fist by his side. Jamie briefly thought it was due to anger until he locked onto those half-lidded eyes filled with passion.

Seth had more sex appeal than any man he'd ever met, but the way he was looking at him made Jamie feel as though he were just as tempting.

"Sir, please."

Loland's quiet plea jerked him back to his lover who was licking his lips, his gaze fixated on the beads of precum glistening on the head of Jamie's cock.

"Do you want that, boy?"

"Yes, Sir. Please, Sir."

Jamie had never heard that note of longing in Loland's voice before. His lover had never needed to beg for any part of his body, but this was Seth's show, and the man dominated every scene in it.

"Put Jamie on the bed and keep your face at his cock. You will not touch it until I give you permission."

Loland licked and nibbled his way up, his hands never breaking contact as he guided Jamie to the middle of the bed. Jamie lay on his back and instinctively pulled up his legs, the heels of his feet almost touching his ass.

From Loland's smile, he guessed he had correctly arranged himself. When Loland crouched over him and assumed the position he'd been instructed to take, Jamie's eyes strayed back to Seth's solid figure standing at the foot of the bed.

Seth reached out to Loland's ass with both hands, digging into his flesh until Loland gasped. "The paddle or my hand, boy. Choose quickly."

"Your hand please, Sir. I need to feel you." Loland's hot breath fanned over the head of his prick and he reached down to ease his throbbing member, but Seth was faster. He twisted around Loland and grabbed Jamie's wrists, pulling them above his head and holding them there with one hand while he leaned in close to his face. The force Seth used to keep him in place was almost bruising. A fresh wave of lust brought his hips up involuntarily and when the tip of his cock brushed Loland's lips, words spilled before he could catch them.

"Please, let go. I can't do this. I can't take it. Too much..."

Without turning his gaze from Jamie, Seth said, "Hold him down. Take his cock into your mouth and let him know how beautiful he is. Make him feel every ounce of pleasure he deserves."

Jamie felt Loland's hands clamp down on his hips a second before his cock was engulfed in searing heat. A cry was torn from his throat and he struggled against their hold, but that only caused them to increase the pressure.

Seth pulled his head back but he didn't relinquish the lock of his gaze or the crushing weight of his hand. A loud smack of flesh on flesh echoed through the room and Loland was pushed forwards, forced to swallow more of his aching cock. Another and another followed, each one pulling a grunt from Loland that vibrated through Jamie's groin. The eyes above him darkened to a deep grey and a tongue darted out to moisten full lips.

Jamie wanted those lips to take possession of his, to devour him until he couldn't breathe, but he needed something else. Something more. He writhed against his bondage, begging to be released but silently praying that it would never end. He could feel the impact of Seth's other hand, as it slapped Loland's ass and upper thighs, throughout his entire body. The rhythm was steady and strong, and the relentless desire on Seth's face told him that the man was showing no mercy.

Loland's grunts turned to long, tortured moans. The mixture of his pain and arousal hummed over Jamie's skin, taking him to heights he'd never known existed before, but still he needed more. Loland's head bobbed with the tempo of the blows to his backside, his cheeks hollowing with the force of his suction around Jamie's cock every time he came up. The sensation created darts of lightning that shot through his legs and chest, and his eyes rolled back into his head.

"No. Look at me. I want to see how sexy you are. You will hide nothing from me."

More words tumbled from Jamie's mouth, faster than he could keep track of them, but he hoped they conveyed his feelings. "Sir, harder, please. I need so much. Don't let me go. I need…"

"Boy, you can touch yourself, but you will not come until you suck the orgasm out of our little one. Give him what he needs. Make him feel it."

Suddenly, everything increased in intensity. Loland released one of his hips but the hand on his other dug in so tightly that he could feel nails biting into his skin. The slam of Seth's strikes to his lover's ass pushed the head of his cock to the back of Loland's throat so that every swallow was strained. The pressure caused Jamie's balls to tighten as they prepared for his release. The grip on his wrists passed the point of pain and he could no longer move his fingers.

"Come. Now."

That was all it took. Jamie convulsed beneath the fierce demand in that tone. A scream was ripped from his throat as his orgasm seized his body, driving long spurts of cum down Loland's willing throat. The low growl that shook the tender nerves of his pulsing prick signalled his lover's climax, causing several ripples of pleasure to fly through him until he thought he would pass out from lack of oxygen.

It took countless minutes for him to float back to reality and the awareness that Loland had collapsed on top of him. Somehow he'd lost the hold of Seth's eyes and missed that connection, but he couldn't gather the will to raise his head to find it again. Loland was still panting hard against him, tickling the fine hairs on his belly.

A yearning took root in the pit of his stomach and he realised that he was still in need. He didn't think it was possible after the stimulation he was continuing to recover from, but there was also an emptiness inside that would not be denied.

He called out without thought. "Master?"

"Right here, baby." And he was. His face came into view and a warm cloth caressed his chest as Seth proceeded to clean Loland's hand and chest. His lover mumbled something unintelligible but was snoring by the time Seth had finished. Jamie shared a tiny smile with him and watched as Seth threw the washcloth to a hand-basket on the floor and lifted first Loland, then Jamie towards the head of the bed.

Jamie wasn't able to bite back his whimper when Seth's arms let him go.

A low chuckle sounded in his ears. "I'm not going anywhere, little one. Let me just get the covers."

Heat suffused Jamie's face. The blanket was laid over them and Seth's long arms reached around him and pulled Loland's body against Jamie's front while Seth spooned him from behind. The rock-hard length of Seth's cock pressed into the crevice of his ass and he tensed.

"Master, you still need."

Another chuckle trickled down his spine. "I got what I wanted. You're gorgeous when you come, do you know that?"

"I...thank you, Sir." It wasn't enough to express the depth of his emotions, but more just seemed superfluous.

"You're welcome. Goodnight, sweeting."

Sweeting. The endearment crept into Jamie's being as he fell into a dreamless sleep.

Chapter Seven

Seth couldn't decide which of his mates was more amusing — the one who constantly squirmed on the pillow on his seat, trying to find a position that didn't aggravate his tender backside, or the one who was madly in love with his collection of books in the study. And while he was glad that Jamie felt more relaxed around him, Seth was beginning to wonder if his appetite had always been poor.

He would eat barely a quarter of each meal and had only partaken of coffee this morning. When Jamie had stated that allowing Seth to feed him as he did Loland was a hard limit, Seth hadn't thought much of it, but now he was beginning to wonder at the reason behind it.

In between answering questions about his books on ancient Rome, he asked, "Jamie, why don't you eat some of your breakfast? It's getting cold."

Jamie ducked his head, black strands hiding his face as he pushed more food around with his fork. "I'll eat later. Anyone want more coffee?"

He got up, but Seth reached out and grabbed his arm as he walked past, mindful of the bruises ringing his wrist. "Eat now. It's not healthy to drink so much coffee on an empty stomach."

Anger contorted Jamie's face and he wrenched his arm away. "Just because I call you Master doesn't mean you can force me to do what you want." He slammed his mug on the counter so hard that the liquid sloshed over the rim and he stomped out of the room.

"I'm sorry," Loland said. "I've never been able to get him to eat much. I think it's a way for him to maintain control of a part of his life. I'll go after him."

"No. I have an idea. Stay here and finish your breakfast but don't clean anything. I'll get it when I get back. I want you to take it easy today. Nothing more strenuous than researching for your trip, okay?"

Loland smiled and leaned in to the kiss Seth planted on his temple. "Yes, Sir. Thank you."

Seth nodded and went in search of his wayward mate. He found Jamie in the study at his computer, typing furiously.

He walked over to his desk but kept a safe distance, not wanting to drive him away again. "Jamie, I apologise if I came across as demanding. I'm worried about your appetite, but it's your choice on when or if you want to tell me why you won't eat."

Jamie's only acknowledgement of his words was a tightening around his eyes.

"I'd like to show you something. Come outside with me." In the five days that Jamie and Loland had been living with him, Jamie had yet to leave the house of his own volition, let alone express interest in the idea.

"I'm working. You know, that thing some of us do to support ourselves? Not all of us can enjoy the luxury of being rich."

Seth sighed. He definitely had his work cut out for him. He knelt down beside Jamie's chair, deliberately putting himself below the other man's height. Jamie was so small that Seth had no doubt his stature was often a sore spot for him. Jamie's hands stilled over the keys and Seth saw the slight tremble in them. When he touched two fingers lightly to the bruises on his wrist, reminding the man of the passion they'd shared the night before, Jamie's face crumpled.

His mate seemed as fragile as thin glass at times, yet displayed such strength at others. It was one of the things Seth admired most about him. Not many people could walk away from all of the trials Jamie had been through in his life and still value their independence.

"I'm not going to pretend to know what you've gone through, but I do want to help you."

"He told you, didn't he?" Jamie whispered.

"I know that you were admitted to a mental hospital. Probably because you were never taught to control your power. Loland said that you were…hurt by a man while you were there, and that he got you out as soon as he was able."

An echo of Jamie's earlier anger played across his face and there was an edge to his voice. "The lies that man told the doctors kept me on drugs that took away my ability to eat, or talk, or move. He controlled me that way for years. Only Lo believed me, but he couldn't stop him from coming to me. From making me do what he wanted."

Jamie's voice grew quieter. "Whenever my weight dropped below a certain point, they would force-feed me. They thought I was trying to starve myself, but I wasn't. It was him. I know that you're different, and I may be a submissive, but I'll never accept that kind of control. I eat when I want, go where I want to and I don't care if you hate me for anything I say."

Seth worked to hide his grin at the man's words. There was so much fire and willpower packed in such a vibrant package. He was relieved beyond measure that Jamie was able to distinguish the difference between domination and abuse. Many survivors never got that far.

"Fair enough. I'll warn you now that I can get a little overbearing when it comes to the people I care about, but I promise to always listen."

Jamie looked down at the fingers still resting on his skin. He was silent for a long while, the pain in his blue eyes receding with each minute that passed. Seth waited. They had centuries ahead of them, an eternity to discover how to make each other happy.

"Why? You have Loland. Lo...loves you. You don't need me to keep his affection. You have it. I promise I won't get jealous or come between you two."

"You really have no idea of how precious you are, do you?"

Jamie's eyes widened in surprise and Seth held his gaze, wanting his mate to see the depth of his sincerity.

"Come with me, please. I want to show you a part of me."

"Fine."

His answer lacked all enthusiasm, but he'd take what he could get. Jamie followed him out of the study and through the kitchen to the heavily-curtained glass doors that led to his garden. He was glad to see the mess cluttering the table and countertops. It meant that Loland had obeyed his command. Seth opened the door and gestured for Jamie to precede him, but his little mate stopped in the doorway.

"I need to put on some clothes."

"It's all right. This house lies in the middle of a considerable stretch of land and this back area is protected from view by a privacy fence in addition to the one around the perimeter."

Jamie bit his lower lip and hesitated for a few more seconds before stepping outside. He didn't get far before he stopped to gape at the bounty of vegetation spilling over the flagstones and stretching towards the sky.

Despite the damage his abuse of power had caused during his fit of rage, the more delicate flowers and leaves were already beginning perk up. His sanctuary appeared no less breathtaking to the untrained eye, and Seth's pride in his diligence in keeping his garden thriving was rewarded by Jamie's reverence.

He watched as his mate walked a circuit of the enclosed area, touching and murmuring gentle words to each and every plant that still needed healing. He'd had a hunch Jamie had been using nature as an outlet for the energy his body involuntarily collected, but he was still awed by the power the man displayed.

Aquene was one of the most skilful Keepers of nature Seth had ever met. Yet even his talent for distributing energy among failing plants while absorbing a measure of his own couldn't compare to Jamie's ability.

A whisper, a touch, even the faint waft of Jamie's breath revived all that he came into contact with. Seth could sense that Jamie didn't have the stores of energy it would normally take to invigorate such a large number of plants at once.

A Keeper could only expend the energy he or she had already accrued in order to dole it out to the plant life around them. The practice of revitalising nature was rarely done because the energy one needed to expend usually exceeded the amount they took in. It would be similar to one human trying to provide enough carbon monoxide for a greenhouse full of plants.

It took some time for realisation to set in, but once it did, Seth found himself speechless. His mate was actually pulling energy from the plant and animal life spanning the entirety of his land and using it to replenish himself as well as the wilted plants within Seth's garden. Yet, as far as Seth knew, it was impossible for a Keeper to absorb energy from living things at the distance his mate was reaching. At more than five hundred years of age, Seth was still unable to stretch his field of absorption past a twenty yard range.

He made a note to enquire about this anomaly the next time he spoke with Aquene. An hour had passed before Loland joined Seth on the back porch.

"Amazing, isn't he, Sir?"

"You've no idea. I know that you're unaware of the scope of the power Jamie and I possess, but his ability far exceeds mine. I've never seen anything like it."

"It may have something to do with his other powers. I was kind of hoping you could help him with those, too."

A chill raced down Seth's spine. "Please tell me you're speaking in terms of his personality."

Loland's bark of laughter didn't ease the anxiety curling in his chest. "As much as I love him, I wouldn't call his personality a power, although it can be pretty...potent...when he wants it to be."

"So what are his other powers?"

Loland didn't answer immediately. His expression as he regarded Jamie was one that Seth had seen on the faces of parents who loved their children, but had no clue as to how to address their specific needs.

Time passed and Seth was beginning to think that Loland wouldn't answer him, then finally Loland asked, "Is it okay if Jamie gives you the answer to that? I don't mean to keep secrets, but I'm afraid that he might become skittish — well...more so than he already is — if I volunteer any more information on him. It's important to me that he stay safe here with you while I'm gone."

Before he could agree, the topic of their conversation swayed on the balls of his feet before plummeting head first into a bed of lilacs and tulips. Both men ran at top speed but Seth reached him first...just after his head collided with the cement leg of a bench in the near left corner of the garden.

Alarm shot through Seth as he nimbly lifted the slight form into his arms and strode towards the door leading to the kitchen, with Loland close behind. Jamie's eyes were dilated and unfocussed and blood poured from the gash on his forehead, but Seth took comfort in the steady pulse he found under the pale skin of his throat. He rushed to the downstairs bathroom and sat on the toilet seat while he instructed Loland to dampen a washcloth.

Loland quickly complied and when Seth pressed the warm cloth to Jamie's temple, his little mate suddenly came alive in a flurry of frightened words and flailing limbs.

"He's coming! He's coming. Let me go. Have to get away."

"Jamie!" Seth shouted, but it did no good. Jamie continued to fight him. He was reminded of the man's nightmare the night he'd gone to collect his mates, but this didn't make any sense. As far as he knew, flashbacks didn't provoke this kind of reaction.

In small increments, Seth began to pull Jamie's energy from him. He didn't take as much as he had last time, not wanting to deplete him to the point of exhaustion. Questions needed to be answered, and the sooner the better.

Loland cleaned and bandaged the head wound once Jamie became subdued enough to let him work. Ten minutes later, a lucid Jamie was staring up at him out of a boyish face with the eyes of an ancient. It was a little off-putting to see someone so gorgeous looking so lost and wary.

"That's it. I'm cancelling my trip."

"No!" Jamie and Seth exclaimed at the same time. Seth reluctantly let go of his mate when he tried to stand and go to Loland, but the moment he wobbled to the side, Seth pulled him right back down into his lap. It earned him a peeved glare but that was much preferable to the possibility of another injury.

"Lo, you have to go. I'm sorry I scared you. It was just..."

"A vision. That's what it was. And don't underplay this. Before, it was always in your sleep and I thought you were just having nightmares about being attacked by that asshole, but you and I both know that your visions always come true. I'm sorry I doubted you, but I can't ignore it anymore. I'm staying."

Jamie tried again to stand up but Seth only strengthened the band of his arms around his midsection. Jamie twisted his head around to stare him in the eye and growled.

Coming from a man who didn't have Jamie's youthful looks or slight stature, it might have been intimidating, but that wasn't the case. Seth had never seen anything cuter in his life. He was laughing out loud before he could stop himself.

Loland joined in and the tension of the moment was broken. The look on Jamie's face said he didn't find it as amusing. Seth was tempted to push his limits just to see if he could get another growl out of him but decided not to push his luck.

"I'm sorry, little one, but you're absolutely adorable when you do that."

Jamie frowned and looked to Loland who chuckled and said, "He's right, you are."

Letting out an irritated huff, Jamie crossed his arms over his chest and mumbled, "And they say I'm crazy."

"Well, if I'm to believe that you're not, would someone mind explaining to me what exactly happened back there?"

Both men shut down immediately.

"Loland?"

Loland shuffled his feet and looked everywhere but at him. He was about to make his question a demand when the man finally spoke up. "I'm sorry, Sir, but I think that's something Jamie needs to tell you himself."

"Jamie?"

"What?"

His belligerent tone was a reflection of more than just his stubbornness. It was a challenge. Seth had heard it in his subs before. It had always reminded him of children who sought out attention in the only way they knew how — by defying authority and breaking the rules. The fact that most subs with this attitude had experienced some kind of trauma in their past was no coincidence.

The effort of teaching them obedience while respecting their boundaries was no easy task, especially when the sub was reluctant to give the Dom necessary information to keep them safe—as was the case in Jamie's situation. But that was far from a deterrent to Seth.

Loland had been giving Jamie comfort and safety to the best of his abilities for years and still had not been able to convince the man of his own self-worth. There was only one way in which Seth felt confident in dealing with Jamie, and he prayed to the Gods that it would work as it had for him previously.

"Boy, you have a portfolio of your work right?"

Loland sent him a confused look. "I have a website that Jamie helped me create. It's got presentations of the work I've done independently as well as for my company on it."

Seth didn't bother to hide his surprise at the accomplishments of both of his mates. "Very good. Go to the study and pull it up. Place copies of your presentations in a separate folder then wait in the living room until Jamie and I join you."

Loland's confusion increased but he obeyed without question. "Yes, Sir."

Once they were alone, Seth lifted Jamie from his lap and sat him down on the toilet seat. For the second time that day, Seth lowered himself in front of Jamie to give his mate a semblance of control.

"I'll make you a deal."

Jamie narrowed his blue gaze and tensed every muscle in his body. He was so ready to expect the worst of every situation. "I'm listening."

"For every bit of information I give you of myself, you will return the favour. With each new piece that I offer, I will demand a rule that you must follow. For each piece that you give to me, you can demand a limit. I will obey your limits and you will obey my rules. If at any point you need your space to think things over, I expect you to use your safe word, but in this context, that will only buy you time. One day. After that, you will give me an answer that is only the whole truth. No hidden innuendos. No white lies."

Seth watched a slew of emotions play across Jamie's face. Fear. Suspicion. Defiance. "You still haven't told me yet why I'm so important to you. You have Loland."

"And I need you as well."

"Why?"

"I'll answer that as soon as you agree to my terms."

"I won't allow you to control me."

"And you already know that a sub holds more control than a Dom. A true dominant is nothing without the gift that only a submissive can offer."

"You have all the answers, don't you?"

"No, sweeting. I'm going about this the only way I know how. It's not perfect, and I have no idea of whether it will work or not, but it's all I've got. I'm kind of hoping that you'll meet me halfway, here."

Seth didn't know which part of that he'd got right, but he was glad all the same for the slow smile that curved Jamie's sexy lips.

"Okay, that was good. I agree to your terms, but…" Jamie bowed his head in embarrassment. His raven locks hid his expression from Seth's view. He reached up and gathered the silken hairs in his hands, lifting them up and away so that his mate's face was bared to him. He placed his palms on either side of the man's head, holding him immobile.

Uncertainty flashed in those large, clear blue eyes and a pink tongue slid seductively over a full bottom lip. "So beautiful," Seth whispered before he urged that lip down to his, biting and licking until Jamie opened up with a gasp.

Seth took full advantage, pressing his mouth firmly to his mate's and denying him the chance to draw in air. He could only compare the torrent of sensation that flushed through him to the first time he had kissed Loland.

But this was different. Loland had been willing, yet averse to settling for anything less than what he wanted. Jamie's kiss was akin to the taming of a wild cat. Wary yet rife with hidden promise. His blood sang with the prospect of gentling the skittish creature he held between his hands. The urge to take the man right there was almost more than he could handle. Breathing heavily, he pulled away from Jamie before the man made him forget all of his carefully cultivated control.

To his deep satisfaction, he watched as Jamie struggled in an attempt to control his own hormones. A glance down at the swollen cock jutting towards him bolstered his ego even more.

"I believe you were about to ask a question?" Seth prompted, a hint of humour in his voice.

Jaime blushed and asked in a small voice, "Am I going to be punished again?"

Seth let his head fall back and laughed. "While your belligerence leaves a lot to be desired, I won't punish you for it this time. I think this situation has been stressful on all of us." He stood up and offered his hand to lead Jamie to the living room.

Chapter Eight

Seth hung up the phone, confident that the first part of his plan would come together without too many complications, then left his study to join his mates in the living room. Loland had assumed his position of attention next to the recliner, while Jamie sat in the very corner of the couch diagonal from the chair.

His cock jerked at the sight of Loland's toned, naked form, standing erect and patiently awaiting his command. If not for the more pressing matter at hand, he'd have his sexy boy bent over the arm of the chair while he pounded his cock so far up his ass, he wouldn't be able to sit still for the next week.

Jamie glanced nervously at him as he sat down. Loland moved to kneel at his feet but he shook his head. "Go sit next to our little one for now." Seth then took the time to fill Loland in on the terms of the agreement he and Jamie had arranged. Loland kept his gaze locked on Jamie's forlorn form, as though he were trying to gauge his stand on the situation, but Jamie gave nothing away.

"Would you like to start, or should I?"

Jamie gave a noncommittal shrug. It was nothing less than what he had expected. "All right. I'll go first then. Ask me a question you'd like to know."

Jamie thought for a second then said, "You said that you have the same powers I do. What does that make us?"

"I get the impression that you have more than one power. If that's true, then I only share one of them. We are Keepers. Immortal beings that possess the ability to absorb energy from every type of life form — plant, animal or human. This gift can invigorate us and it is what gives us immortality and extra strength, depending on the amount of energy we've accumulated. I am, for instance, over five hundred years old. It becomes necessary, however, to disperse most of that energy once it builds up to a certain point within us.

"When that happens, we offer it to our Gods, who in turn use it to revitalise themselves. They are, in essence, servants to us just as we are to them. We are co-dependent upon each other and therefore strive to work together."

It was a vast concept and one that most fledglings had a hard time comprehending even with the informal training their parents provided them while growing up. Seth studied Jamie's reaction carefully, expecting the typical barrage of ensuing questions most trainees bombarded him with. It never came.

Loland gaped openly but Jamie simply nodded his head and spoke without raising his eyes from his hands. "And your rule?"

His desolate countenance was beginning to frighten Seth, but he couldn't change the policies now. He had instigated this game. It was his responsibility to follow through with it. He decided to go with the least demanding of his stipulations.

"I want you to allow me to show you what it means to be a Keeper. This is my job. This huge house, the extensive lands and bottomless bank funds I have, they all serve the same purpose. The Goddess of Fate informs me of any Keepers old enough to go through training, and I either go to them or welcome them into my home. I show them how to safely absorb the energy they come into contact with every day and how to use it to give to our Gods when the time comes. This training will eventually require you to go out in public, but I'll be with you the whole time."

Anger suffused Jamie's features. "So you try to fuck every initiate you take in?"

The question provoked his own rage at the misguided assumption and he was not happy with the amount of effort it took to control his own response. He'd dealt with the unruliness of fledglings before and he should be able to kerb his temper by now.

"That is the answer to a question you've asked out of turn. Will you abide by my rule?"

Jamie let out a growl and Seth growled right back. The show of dominance from his mate brought his forgotten arousal back to life. *Damn, the man was sexy!*

"Yes," Jamie reluctantly answered.

"Good. Now please tell me about your other power."

"Which one?" Jamie arched a cocky brow.

Fuck. Well didn't that just put the icing on the cake. "How many others are there?"

"Is that a separate question?"

"Boy, I will strip you down and take you to the dungeon for a whipping."

"Fine. I'll take that as my limit. One of my powers is precognition."

Did he just...? Seth stared at his mate, dumbfounded by his manipulation. "You want me to whip you?" Seth had already eliminated that possibility due to Jamie's past abuse.

"I...yeah. I mean...unless you don't want to. I...I'm sorry. Lo?" The sudden dive that Jamie's confidence took was just as confusing as its appearance, but Seth refused to let the opportunity slip by.

"Done. Now I'm sure I don't need to warn you to..."

"To use my safe word if things go too far," Jamie finished for him. "You're getting predictable in your old age."

The little shit. "We'll see how predictable I am when I have you bent over the spanking bench, boy."

Loland burst out laughing and Jamie's grin stretched from ear to ear, but they were both sporting rock-hard erections.

Seth chuckled. "Okay, back to business. The episode in the garden — was that an effect of your precognition?"

"Yes. When I have a vision, my senses are transferred to it. Hearing, sight, sound, touch. It all becomes a part of the vision. Most times, though, I just know things. Like intuition. I knew two weeks after you and Loland met that you were the one for him so you can tell him you love him now. Besides, it's not like it isn't disgustingly obvious." Jamie's eyes twinkled with mischief.

Loland smacked him on the back of the head. "Brat! Why didn't you tell me that?"

"Ow. 'Cause it would have been like giving away the twist at the end of a movie. You hate that."

Loland looked at Seth dreamily. "Yeah, you're right. The journey was definitely half the fun."

Seth felt a breathtaking surge of happiness fill his being. He wanted to say the words, but at the same time, he wanted to wait until he could say them to Jamie as well. "That it was. Let's move on to the next question. Jamie?"

"Why do you want me when you have Loland?"

He'd known this was coming. He paused to think of the best way to phrase his answer. It wasn't just Jamie's response he had to deal with, but Loland's as well. After a long silence, he decided that he would have to trust in the blunt truth and hope that they didn't run screaming from the house.

"You know that intense feeling, that powerful rush you get whenever I'm in your presence?" Both men looked at each other, then at him, and nodded. "That's because you are my mates. You both are."

"You mean mate as in destined lovers? As in the one person you're meant to spend the rest of your life with, 'mate'?"

An unfamiliar lump of trepidation clogged his throat as he first met the gaze of a curious brown set of eyes, then a wary blue set. "Yes. That's exactly what I mean. Each Keeper is destined to have a mate to stay with them, love them throughout their life. One person that contains the qualities that will be a perfect match for that Keeper. I don't know why, but I was gifted with two mates. I knew it from the moment I met each of you."

"So you have no choice but to accept me?" Jamie asked. The bleakness in his voice nearly tore a seam in Seth's heart.

"No, little one. We may have been born with compatible qualities, but it doesn't mean that I'm your only option. You are immortal, just as I am, and Loland is your mate, just as he is mine." Seth looked over at Loland's incredulous stare. "The energy that we, as Keepers, collect would keep you sustained for as long as you live, no matter who you chose to live with. If you chose to live with someone else, or by yourself, you would eventually die of old age."

Silence ruled the room.

After what seemed an eternity, Loland cleared his throat and asked, "How do you feel about this, Sir?"

A slow smile spread across his face until he was grinning like an idiot. "I've been waiting for my mate for over five hundred years. Finding out I have two just makes it that much sweeter. I have to admit, it's very unusual. I've never heard of a Keeper having more than one mate. I called a friend to see if he could give me some information as to why, but now that I've got to know you both, I don't think I care so much anymore.

"He's very jealous, by the way, although I've met his mate before. I'm not so sure he would think of himself as lucky if he had two of her. She's—" *How to put this delicately?* "—well, a handful. I'll be training their six sons when they're ready, so I'm sure you'll get to meet them all soon." *If you're still with me.* He kept that last part to himself. The thought that they might choose to leave was one he couldn't entertain right now.

Jamie wore a pained expression on his face and when he spoke it was with a great deal of hesitation. "If I say 'red' on the whole…mate…thing, can I have more than a day to think about it? I'm not saying no, I just…I need some time to wrap my head around the idea. Is that okay?"

It was more than okay. It was more than he'd expected, considering he'd only known Jamie for roughly one week. "Of course. Both of you take as much time as you need. I'll respect whatever decisions you make."

Loland squeezed Jamie's thigh. "Thank you, Sir. I know this can't be easy for you either."

Seth shrugged. For him, this *was* the easy part. It would only get hard if he were forced to spend years convincing them that he was worth their love.

"So, I guess you get another rule," Jamie said.

Ah, the silver lining. "I want you to start working out with me. I have a few exercise machines here but I prefer to go to the gym. I can start you on a regimen and help you when you need it." The man wasn't in bad shape, but working out would build his appetite, which was the main purpose of this rule.

"I'm twenty-two, not two. I can take care of myself. Am I the only one that hears me when I say that?"

His mate's quick-flash temper was definitely going to take some getting used to. "This isn't about how well you can manage your life. It's about developing focus. Exercise will help with that. All Keepers need to learn it to some degree, but I think you would especially benefit from it because of your extra power."

The conflict on Jamie's face to keep from arguing against his logic was almost comical. "Can I do it here?"

"Yes. As part of your training, we'll go to the gym a few times, but for the most part you can stay here."

If Jamie growled again, Seth wasn't sure he would be able to keep from laughing, but the sexy man just huffed and gave his habitual, "Fine," response. This was turning out to be more rewarding than he'd anticipated.

"Good, then. Now tell me about your other power. Is this the last one?"

"Yeah." Jamie squirmed again and glanced over at Loland. The other man nodded his head in encouragement but it still took a few minutes for Jamie to gather his courage. Seth had the feeling he wasn't going to like the answer. "I can...see when a person is close to death. They have an aura about them, kind of like a dark film that covers their skin. It's what landed me in the hospital." Jamie shuddered. "I told my foster parent at the time that his wife was going to die. He didn't like that."

Cold dread filled him as the pieces to the puzzle of Jamie finally fell into place. The clues had been there all along, but he had been so fixated on the possible danger his mate might be in to take notice. Raised by humans. Possessing multiple powers. Kept secret from him. Apparently allotted to die some time ago. A second mate.

Jamie's very existence was based on a lie. He was taboo in his world. *Their* world. The Gods would kill him if they found out about him. And the Goddess of Fate had known all along. As had Aquene. Why else would the man warn him to keep Jamie from communicating with their Gods?

No wonder Jamie had taken to the idea of immortality so easily. He'd dealt with more than his fair share of oddities throughout his entire life.

"Sir?"

Loland's voice was distant. He looked over at the man and realised that his own hands were clenched so tightly his knuckles were straining against his skin. It couldn't be. Loland had been a miraculous gift, but in the short time since he'd met Jamie, his other mate had quickly become just as important to him. If he lost Jamie, he would lose them both. Loland would never recover. At this point, he was pretty sure that he wouldn't either.

"Please excuse me. I need to make a phone call." He rose from his chair but was stopped by Jamie.

"Wait. You need to call someone now? I'm not that stupid. You're going to tell someone what I just told you, aren't you?" Fear and anger warred on Jamie's face and his body began to shake.

Seth didn't know what to say but he couldn't bring himself to lie. He didn't want to destroy the fragile trust they'd begun to establish. Then again, it didn't seem as though Jamie would readily forgive him for exposing his secret, even if it was for his own good.

He sat down again, but this time on the coffee table in front of the couch so he could look his mate in the eye. He took one of Jamie's trembling hands in his and held it firmly. His mate looked ready to bolt and Seth realised he would have to keep physical contact with him until he was sure Jamie wouldn't try to run. If he was correct in his assumption, Jamie was going to need all the protection he could get.

"I'm only going to tell my friend, Aquene, and only because I trust him enough to keep your powers confidential. He's a Keeper, like us. Jamie, you could be in very real danger because of your abilities. I need more information in order to better protect you."

"Bullshit! I don't believe you. You going to try to have me committed, aren't you?"

"No, and watch your tone, boy. This is more serious than you realise."

"You're trying to get rid of me."

"I'm trying to save your life!" Seth yelled. Jamie shot up and fought against his hold, pulling Seth up with him. With surprising speed, the other man threw a punch towards his head but Seth ducked away before it could connect with his jaw. He yanked Jamie to him, catching him in both arms when he lost his balance.

A sharp pain flared up his leg and into his groin from a kick that came dangerously close to his testicles. Back to chest, he held his mate to him, drawing out just enough energy to lessen his struggles.

"Enough!" Loland's roar shocked them both into immobility. "What the hell is going on? Why is he all of a sudden in danger now? Is it because he met you?"

The accusation in Loland's voice cut deeply. "Not exactly. I promise to tell you everything I know, but I need you both to give me the chance to do that. Please."

Loland deliberated for a moment then walked around to face Jamie. Seth released his wrist but retained his tight hold. The hug Loland gave the smaller man was awkward, given the position in which he held Jamie, but Seth wasn't willing to let go just yet.

"Baby, I think we should listen to what he has to say. Your dreams of being hunted are turning into visions and you know that ignoring them won't make them go away. I can't lose you." He pulled away to look at him and gently stroke the bandage on Jamie's brow. "I made a promise years ago that I would never let you go back to a mental ward. If you can't trust Seth, then please trust me. We'll figure this out. Together."

Jamie pulled forwards and at first, Seth thought that he might be trying to get free of him again, but the painful sob that filled the silence explained his movement. Seth's embrace instantly changed from one of detainment to one of comfort. Loland wrapped his own arms around Jamie again, including Seth in his embrace. They stood there holding their mate between them for countless minutes while he unburdened his fears through tears and racking sobs.

Surprisingly, Seth now thought that the impact of what he was going to have to tell Jamie later, once he got confirmation from Aquene, would be easier for the man to take than what he was going through now. Abandonment seemed to be Jamie's worst fear, and if they could get past that, they would stand a much better chance at coming up with a solution to their predicament.

Seth felt Jamie's body go limp and he surrendered his hold on the wilted form of his mate to Loland, guiding them both to the couch. Jamie eventually lapsed into an exhausted numbness against Loland, and Seth wiped away the drying tracks of his tears.

"I'll be right back, just let me grab my cell phone from the kitchen." He was back in less than a minute, phone in hand and dialling Aquene's number. Seth put it on speaker so his mates could listen in on the conversation. His friend picked up on the second ring.

"Tell me you still have him there with you," Aquene spoke first.

"I do. You knew he was the son of a God all along, didn't you?"

Two pairs of perplexed eyes immediately locked onto him.

"No, but I had a hunch. I got some information yesterday that lent credence to my theory, though nothing conclusive about your mate. You sound certain, though. What happened?"

Seth pinched the bridge of his nose. "I should have guessed sooner. He was brought up among humans and has more powers than any Keeper I know of."

"Such as?"

"He has precognition, visions. He can also discern when people are about to die. Any idea on which God may have sired or given birth to him?"

There was a lengthy pause on the other end. He could feel the anxiety in the room mounting with each second that passed. Jamie sat up and Seth moved close, prepared to go another round if the man attempted to run again, but their mate remained seated.

He was about to ask again when Aquene said, "I'm on my way now. If it's all right with you, I'm going to have Jace and Malen join us at your house. I trust them and they might know some others who can help. We'll figure everything out when we get there."

"I have no problem with that, but I want an answer. You know who it is, don't you?"

A gruff sigh sounded before his friend grudgingly replied, "I'm not absolutely certain, but I think it may be the God of Death. That last power of your mate's fits his talents and from what I was able to learn, Death has yet another son out there but no one can get a fix on his location. Only Fate and a handful of Keepers know about him."

"How the hell has he been able to keep the existence of two offspring from the other Gods?"

"I don't know, at least not yet. I'll call the others and jump on the first plane out of here. We should all be there by morning. In the meantime, don't let either of your mates out of your sight. We don't want to take the risk of Loland being used as leverage if anyone else figures out Jamie's identity."

"Yeah. Thanks man. We'll see you soon."

"Count on it. And, Seth... Don't stress out over this too much. I haven't spent centuries saving your ass only to lose you to the loss of your mate. We'll keep him safe."

The confidence in Aquene's voice bolstered his own, but they still had a long road ahead of them. "I can't promise anything, but I'll try to keep that in mind."

He ended the call but wouldn't meet the stares of his mates until he was able to mask the panic inside. He needed to focus.

"As you heard, we'll be having company soon, so you two will go back to wearing clothes for the duration of their stay. Loland, I've already sent the folder with your profile to a friend of mine who's also a decorator. She helped me design my garden and will be able to find you all the work you want in case your boss doesn't take kindly to you backing out of the job in Vegas. I'm sorry, but it looks like you'll have to stay here after all. I have no idea when we'll be able to get this situation resolved."

"What situation?" Jamie asked.

Oh Gods. How could he expect his mates to grasp the scope of the danger they were in when he could barely comprehend it himself? No matter how delicately he worded his response, Jamie was going to be crushed.

And life just got better and better.

Chapter Nine

Seth sat back down on the coffee table. "We think that you're the son of the God of Death and a Keeper. While affairs between Gods and Keepers are frowned upon, they're not unheard of. To have a child born of that affair, though, is forbidden. The offspring would inherit some of the powers of both parents, making them more powerful than any Keeper and, depending on their gifts, many of the Gods."

Jamie shook his head, brows drawn together. "But if your friend had a hunch about it, then he must have heard of this happening before. What happened to the offspring that time?"

"He, uh... He was killed."

"By who?"

Shit. He didn't want to say this. Didn't even want to think about it. Somehow, saying it would make everything real. Inescapable. Right now, he was still drifting in shock. "The God of Wrath, but only because he got to the boy first. Gods and Keepers alike searched for him once his existence had become known."

"Could the man in my vision be the God of Wrath?"

"I don't know. What does he look like?" Seth had seen the corporeal forms that Death and Wrath took while on earth once or twice, so he would be able to differentiate by the description.

"Almost as tall as you. Big build. Black hair and eyes. He has a scar on the side of his face from his brow to his left ear."

"No. The corporeal forms that the Gods take cannot be scarred, which means we're dealing with someone else."

"If he's the son of a God and possibly has a brother out there, maybe they're trying to find Jamie," Loland piped up. "They could help."

Given the fact that Fate had suggested Jamie's own father should have collected him in death years ago, Seth was betting against those odds. He shook his head grimly.

"So I have a battalion of Gods and Keepers out to kill me."

"It hasn't come to that yet and I won't let it. My friends and I will keep you safe, no matter the cost."

Jamie fell silent. There was nothing in his demeanour to give away how he was processing this information. Externally, Jamie was calm and composed. Internally, Seth was screaming, raging against the injustice of their dilemma.

After some time, Jamie spoke up again. "What if the cost is your life, or Loland's life, or the lives of your friends? I can't be responsible for that."

"Jamie, what are you saying?" There was more than an edge to Loland's voice, and Seth thought he understood why.

"My dreams were warning me. In my vision, the man knew where I was. I can't let you risk your lives..."

"You leave me and I'll kill you myself. How dare you try to make my decision for me!" Loland fumed. "You really think I would let you just waltz out of here to your death without trying to stop you? If I have to lock you up in the dungeon or tie you to the bed, I will. In fact..." He bolted from the couch and marched out of the room and up the stairs.

Jamie turned wide eyes to Seth, but he was just as confused by the man's intentions as Jamie was. A minute later, Loland came back in with one hand held behind his back. He stormed up to Jamie with a furious look and before anyone could react, brought his hidden hand around and clamped a metal bracelet around Jamie's left wrist.

Loland shoved a small key into Seth's hand then glared down at his lover. "There. Now that that's settled, I'm going to make a few rules of my own. I've sat here quietly listening to you two this whole time and I think it's only fair that I get a turn.

"Jamie, you will go nowhere without my or Seth's permission. Seth, you will not lock me away for my own safety simply because I'm human. I've known you long enough to know you'll try that. And if either one of you does anything stupid, like attempt to be a hero and end up getting hurt, I will skin you alive. Got it?"

Seth and Jamie were still staring, dumbfounded, at the handcuffs binding Jamie to Loland. Seth had forgotten he kept those in his bedroom closet. They didn't get much use, due to the potential of damage to the skin of a sub.

He looked at the key in his hand, then back at Loland. *Damn, he loved that man!* "So we're all in this together. I promise not to exclude you from anything. Jamie, do you agree to his rules?"

Jamie curled in on himself but nodded. His black locks fell forwards, hiding his face, and he hunched his shoulders but otherwise showed no display of emotion. It was disconcerting to say the least, but all he could do now was offer protection and support. A plan would have to wait until the others showed up tomorrow.

"Loland, call your boss and let him know you won't be able to make your trip. You'll also need to cancel your current job. Can you find someone to take it over?"

"Already have someone in mind. Should I make us something to eat after that, Sir?"

Seth glanced at his watch. They still had plenty of time to prepare for their company before turning in for the night. "Yes, that would be great. We'll start on the guest bedrooms afterwards." Seth reached out to touch Jamie's cheek but he flinched away. When Loland tried to take his hand, he twisted around and stood up to avoid contact.

"Baby, don't do this," Loland pleaded. "We're only trying to keep you safe."

His only reaction was to withdraw further into himself, his hair now completely hiding his features. Loland sighed and made his way back to the bedroom for his cell phone with his lover in tow.

Seth immediately found a pair of soft leather cuffs with a combination lock to replace the metal ones then set about gathering supplies from his storage room. Since he often hosted trainees at his house, he was always stocked with basic necessities. He made a list of additional groceries and anything else he could think of to accommodate their company, then set it aside for one of the men to take care of later. The risk of leaving his mates alone for even a few hours was just too great to take.

Jamie refused to eat or drink during lunch and though he readily helped with the guest rooms, he remained unresponsive. He continued to shy away from touch. One might think that would be difficult to do while cuffed to another man, but somehow he managed to pull it off.

Dinner was a strained affair as he and Loland tried their best not to demand that Jamie eat his food. Finally, the rigid posture and silence of his mate came to be too much. Tears, anger, even fighting he could deal with, but not this complete withdrawal from communication. He would not save his mate from death only to lose his heart and spirit. Seth felt as though he would lose his own if it came to that.

When Loland rose to clear the dishes, Seth pushed him back down then went to the liquor cabinet. He grabbed the aged Scotch and two glasses, filling one with twice as much liquid as the other. He turned and set them in front of his mates, giving Jamie the fuller glass. He purposefully leaned in close to Jamie on one side, giving the man no choice but to either hold his ground or lean in to Loland on his other side.

"You stated being commanded to eat as a hard limit. I'm going to be manipulative and command you to drink this. I know your stomach is empty, but this isn't enough to inebriate you. Just to help you loosen up a bit."

Jamie held himself stiffly but eyed his glass with suspicion. Seth nodded to Loland who took his cue and gulped down the contents of his own glass. Hesitantly, Jamie followed suit but coughed at the burn of the alcohol. Seth took advantage and grasped Jamie's unshackled hand in his larger one. He pulled him up before he had a chance to recover and dragged them both from the kitchen to the staircase leading down to his dungeon.

Once inside, he closed the door and led his mates to the centre of the room. By this time, Jamie had stopped coughing and was looking about with flushed cheeks and bulging eyes. It was definitely an improvement on his earlier indifference. He knew his vast collection of furniture and toys could be daunting to even an experienced sub, so he could imagine the effect it had on his mates.

Most of his toys were displayed on the walls. It made for easy access and added a measure of humility to his submissives to be in the presence of so many pleasure and torture devices. He hadn't planned on bringing them to this room until they grew more comfortable in their roles as his subs, but Jamie needed a release from his stress now.

He stood tall in front of them and said, "While in this room, you will not speak unless spoken to, and then only to answer a direct question. You are to address me only as Master or Sir, and you will remain in the position I order you to until directed otherwise."

Loland had already assumed his standing position, eyes downcast, back straight, with his hands held behind him and legs spread, but Jamie stared openly at him. He knew his younger mate didn't do it as a challenge, but simply because he was still inexperienced. Seth slowly raised his hand and clasped it around Jamie's throat, pleased when he didn't jerk away.

His fingers gradually tightened, applying an even amount of pressure until he cut off his air flow. "Hold your body straight and lower your eyes. Empty your mind of everything but the desire to please me. I am your Master and I will take care of you, but I need your willing submission."

Jamie's chest began to heave in an attempt to pull air into his lungs but Seth didn't let go until he adjusted his body and his eyelids drooped down. When he released him, Jamie took in great gulps of oxygen but kept his body in formation. A glance down showed him that both men were already hard with anticipation.

"Do not move." Seth pivoted and strode over to a standing oak cabinet and opened its drawers, taking his time in choosing various toys and restraints. He knew Jamie was peeking from beneath his lashes because he could feel a spike of energy shoot from the man every time he pulled out a new object. That was good. It meant his distraction was working.

When he was satisfied with his selection, he returned to his mates and placed everything on a small stand to the side.

He decided to start with Loland and picked up the nipple clamps. Standing in front of him, he rubbed his hands along Loland's chest and sides before bending down to take one dark disc into his mouth. He latched on to it and sucked hard, pulling the blood to the surface and flicking his tongue across the tip. He bit down on the nub and rolled it between his teeth then drew back and blew so that it hardened and a small tremor shook Loland's body.

He repeated the process with the other nipple then pinched them both until he heard a gasp. Quickly, he attached the clamps and tugged on the chain connecting them until Loland whimpered. Next, he picked up the cock ring and handed it to Loland.

"Hold this, boy. Kneel in front of our little one and take his cock into your mouth. Get him ready for the ring but do not put it on until I say so."

Loland took it and lowered himself to his knees, watching his lover's face through his lashes as he swallowed him whole. Jamie jerked and looked down in awe as firm lips buried themselves against his crotch.

Instead of pulling back, Loland swivelled his neck up and down so that the sensitive head of Jamie's cock slid along the muscles in the back of his throat. Seth took one of the butt plugs and a tube of lube then crouched down behind Loland. Jamie's breath hitched as his gaze fixed on the plug. Seth lubricated it and dropped the tube before spreading Loland's cheeks wide with his other hand.

When he pressed the cool tip to Loland's tight, outer ring and began to work it in, Loland moaned and Jamie's eyes flew up to meet Seth's again. Instead of reminding the man to keep his eyes down, Seth held his gaze as he pumped the large plug in and out of Loland's ass before he finally shoved it in all the way.

Loland let out a gargled cry and worked Jamie's cock in and out of his mouth as Seth twisted and turned the flat end of the plug. He kept up his assault until Loland cried out again and bit the soft flesh just beneath the head of Jamie's cock when the plug grazed his prostate. Jamie grunted and jerked again, still held mesmerised by Seth's hard gaze.

Seth stood and lubricated the second butt plug where Jamie could watch him and see what was about to be inside him. When he walked behind Jamie, the man's breathing quickened to sharp pants. Seth laid a soothing hand along the small of his back.

"Relax, baby. I promise I won't hurt you. I want you to listen to my voice." Seth rubbed his palm over Jamie's cheeks before splitting them open and pressing the tip of the plug against his hole. "I'm going to take this nice and slow. Concentrate on the warmth of the mouth sucking on your cock." He lowered his head to Jamie's ear so that his hot breath raised chills along his mate's neck. "Focus on the feel of the plug stretching you wide, driving deeper, filling you until you think you can't take any more."

Loland increased his pace and Seth eased the plug in and out, pressing it in further with each pass and angling it up and down until Jamie's muscles loosened enough to accept the widest part of the bulb. Finally, he pushed until it slid completely inside. Seth paused to give Jamie time to adjust to the invasion, then began to manoeuvre the plug.

Jamie shouted and bucked as Seth found his sweet spot. Seth's cock jerked at the soft cries of his mate as he rubbed the tip over Jamie's nub again and again. He continued his assault until Jamie was trembling and begging for mercy.

"Master, please. I'm going to come. Can't stop…"

"Loland."

His boy immediately abandoned Jamie's pulsing prick and slid the cock ring into place, pulling down on Jamie's ball sack to secure and snap the leather strap around it. Seth reached around and gripped Jamie's cock from behind, squeezing until he whimpered.

"I'll tell you when you can come, little one."

After helping Loland to rise, Seth took hold of the short chain linking their cuffs together and led them to the spanking bench facing the far wall. Once there, he walked behind them and pressed on their shoulders, guiding them down and over the bench so that their chests lay across the padded top, side by side. He circled back to the front and pulled their joined wrists forwards, attaching the chain to a hook on the other side.

While he retrieved two single wrist cuffs from the table, he said, "I know our little one requested to feel the sting of a whip, but I can't decide on that or a paddle." He took Loland's free wrist and bound it in one of the cuffs, then secured it to a hook on his side of the bench. "What do you think, boy?" He repeated the process on the other side to Jamie's wrist while he waited for his answer.

"A paddle, Sir."

"Good choice." A paddle brought down in the centre of Jamie's ass would hit the plug just right, forcing it deeper so that it would graze his prostate every time. He walked over to the wall holding his array of paddles and chose a padded one with three small holes in the middle. By the time he returned, Jamie was panting again, trying to twist his head to keep an eye on Seth.

"Slow your breathing. Remember your safe word. I won't push you further than you can go." He traced the palm of his hand down Jamie's spine, rubbing and speaking soothing words until he felt the man's body gradually relax. "That's it. I want you to enjoy this. Are you okay so far?"

Jamie took several deep breaths. "Yes, Master."

"That's my baby." Taking away his hand, he brought the paddle down with a loud smack, without warning. Jamie cried out in surprise. He landed it again and picked up a steady rhythm, switching from the left to the right side and back again so that Jamie could anticipate the placement of the strikes.

He started out with relatively light taps, then built the force of his swings until Jamie's ass took on a beautiful, bright red flush. Every so often, he aimed the paddle directly over the base of the plug, pulling gasps from Jamie's throat that grew in volume with each carefully placed strike.

Once Jamie began to squirm, Seth switched the paddle to Loland's ass while he messaged Jamie's backside with his other hand, glorying in the satisfying heat. The swats he administered to Loland were harsher, knocking him forwards, pressing his swollen cock against the edge of the bench. He was already familiar with Loland's threshold for pain and delighted in the loud whimpers of his mate.

Loland craved to be pushed to his limits and beyond. It wasn't so much the pain of the blows but the unrelenting force behind them. The trust he had in Seth allowed him to give in to his secret desire to be brought to tears, forced to endure the pain he was dealt in order to please his Master. Loland began to scream and beg for mercy but still Seth kept up the ruthless pounding, letting his boy know how much he pleased him.

When Loland's cries began to lessen and his body lost some of its tension, Seth knew he was reaching his subspace. As much as he wanted to take his boy there, he needed to keep him here, with them. He took the paddle in his other hand and resumed the strokes to Jamie's ass while gliding his palm over Loland's scorching heat.

Jamie instantly began to fight against his restraints as if he realised Seth was deliberately pushing him. Testing his limits.

"Breathe through the pain, little one." He alternated between Jamie's ass and thighs in a steady, strong beat. "I won't let you go. I'm right here. You're safe. I want you to focus on your body, everything that you're feeling." He landed a particularly hard blow on the plug, eliciting a sharp yell from Jamie. "That's it. Let me hear you."

Jamie writhed and bucked, his shouts increasing in volume. Seth started to become concerned, afraid his mate was reaching his breaking point and had forgotten his word to end it. He almost came in his pants when he heard Jamie scream out, "Fuck me. Please Master, please. I need...so much."

Seth threw down the paddle and released Loland's single cuff, then unhooked the chain between their joined wrists. He guided Loland to kneel behind Jamie and whispered in his ear, "Fuck our baby. Give him what he wants."

Loland grabbed onto Jamie's wrist that was cuffed to his own and reached down with his other hand to remove the plug from his hole. Jamie groaned as Loland slid his length slowly into him while bending him further over to accommodate his length. When Loland's cock was buried up to the hilt, he reached his free arm around Jamie's waist and held himself there. After several seconds, he eased his prick back out then shoved forwards again.

Seth waited for as long as he could before he freed his own aching cock from the confines of his pants and yanked the plug from Loland's ass. Before the man had time to gasp, he thrust his cock into his mate's tight hole so hard that Loland slammed even further into Jamie, causing him to scream again.

He set a brutal pace, unable to control his arousal as it swept through him and took over. Each battering thrust from Seth drove Loland's cock mercilessly into Jamie's hole until the smaller man was begging for release.

"Take off the cock ring," Seth gritted through his teeth.

It took Loland a few tries but he knew the moment it fell away when Jamie shouted, "Master!"

"Come!"

Jamie's yell was drowned by Loland's scream. He could only drive himself into the heat surrounding his cock twice more before the clenching of Loland's muscles forced his orgasm to bowl through his body, temporarily stealing his sanity. The spasms surging through him and around his cock held him immobile as he strove to pull air into his lungs. The desperate pants of his mates filled his ears and he revelled in the delicious flow of sexual energy.

A small moan sounded from beneath him, bringing him back to his surroundings. He pulled himself from his mate and took a brief moment to admire the sight below him. Loland had both arms wrapped around Jamie's midsection and his little one's face was turned to the side, a beguiling smile on his lips.

He gave them each a thorough kiss, pouring into them all of the love and appreciation he held in his heart for his mates. Loland returned the kiss and emotions in earnest, as he always did. When Jamie did the same, Seth's head spun with relief and happiness. He couldn't help but feel as though he had won a small victory. He removed the single cuffs and said to Loland, "Go on and take our baby to bed. I'll be up shortly."

Loland turned Jamie in his arms and helped him from the room while Seth cleaned and straightened the dungeon. After a sweep of the locks on the doors and windows throughout the house, he climbed the stairs and found his mates curled around each other in their bed. Jamie was already out, but Loland lifted a corner of the covers in invitation.

He hastily stripped and joined them. When he moved to Loland's side, the man climbed over him so that Seth lay between them, their linked hands resting on his belly.

"How are you feeling, boy?"

Loland snuggled into him and sighed. "I honestly don't know, Sir. I keep thinking I'll wake up tomorrow to find that all I've learned today was part of an elaborate dream. Nightmare, rather. I've been taking care of Jamie for so many years now that the idea of not being able to do so this time scares the crap out of me."

"We'll make it through this alive. All of us."

"I believe you, but you and I both know that death isn't the only way we could lose Jamie."

Yes, he did. If anyone got hurt or died, Jamie would undoubtedly blame himself. It's what he would do if he were in Jamie's shoes. Did Seth think Jamie would be able to recover from that guilt? Most likely not.

"You're right, but we still have him now. We'll just have to keep him here." He feathered his thumb over the delicate features of Jamie's face and smiled when their mate snuggled further into his side.

Loland squeezed him from behind and placed a soft kiss on the nape of his neck. "I do love you, Seth."

He closed his eyes and savoured the warm, peaceful energy radiating from the men surrounding him. "I love you, Loland. And I think I've loved Jamie since he first took that swing at my head with the baseball bat."

Loland giggled. "He has his endearing moments." There was a short pause, then, "He loves you too, you know. I can see it. It may take a while for him to admit his own feelings, even to himself, but they're obvious every time he looks at you."

His heart soared at those words. He'd caught glimpses of what he'd hoped was trust and affection from Jamie, but hadn't yet dared to believe...

"Thank you, baby."

Loland gave him another squeeze and Seth fell asleep wondering what he'd ever done to deserve two such wonderfully amazing mates.

Chapter Ten

Company. Three men talking and laughing with his lover and his...mate...in the living room. Jamie could see their faces as though he were watching them on television beneath the blanket pulled over his head. The glimpse was brief, however, and left him in darkness and silence as it faded.

His wrist was bare where it had previously been shackled to Loland. Did that mean his partner thought him too weak or inept to possibly escape with three additional men in the house?

Jamie didn't think so. As much as he hated the prospect of putting these men in danger, running would only cause them to give chase, which could involve potentially dangerous and unnecessary exposure. He was effectively trapped. Loland and Seth must have come to the same conclusion this morning.

Once in the bathroom, he twisted his body in front of the mirror to inspect his ass. A warm tingle raced up his spine as he took in the colourful bruises. His cock perked up at the first thought that came into his mind — *I belong to him now.* It was irrational and a little presumptive. He had no idea if Seth had done what he did as a form of claiming him, but Jamie couldn't help the small thrill he felt at the idea.

He really didn't want to go downstairs and meet the newcomers, but the thought of being fetched by Loland or Seth like an errant child was even less appealing. With a great amount of reluctance, he took a shower and got dressed. The reminder that Seth's friends were here solely to help keep him safe didn't assuage his anxiety as he silently descended the stairs. He paused just out of sight at the entrance to the living room and listened to get a feel for the conversation.

It sounded as though Seth were reminiscing with his friends. The mood was light but that curious shifting of energy he always felt in Seth's presence was magnified. Loland's usually beaming flow of energy was dampened and Jamie wondered if it was because the other Keepers were absorbing his energy and dividing it among them. This thought propelled him into the room to ensure that they weren't harming his lover.

It didn't appear so. Loland sat at Seth's feet, resting his head on his lap while Seth absently stroked his curls. Two strangers occupied the couch opposite them while a third stood next to the cold fireplace, leaning with his back to the wall, ankles crossed.

Everyone stopped talking the moment they saw him. Jamie felt an irresistible compulsion to flee back to the safety of the bedroom. He took a step back but Seth was there, striding towards him with all the confidence of a knight in shining armour.

He allowed the warmth of Seth's body and his smile to envelop him, temporarily struck by the realisation that, for the first time in his life, he felt safe in the arms of someone other than Loland. Seth kissed him soundly and he melted into his embrace. Arousal raced through his body as he surrendered to the dominance of Seth's tongue and strong hands.

It felt so right, so natural, that he forgot about their audience. He tried to burrow closer against the large chest but Seth broke the kiss and took hold of Jamie's shoulders, turning him to face the strangers.

"Little one, these are the friends I was telling you about. That's Malen in the biker jacket and bandana, the blond is Jace, and the guy with more hair than face is Aquene. Guys, this is Jamie."

Jamie flattened himself against Seth's chest when the two men from the couch stood and all three walked towards them. The biker had long, black hair tamed by a bandana with a white skull and flames on it. He was tall. Taller than Seth by at least a few inches, but slimmer. His muscles were plain to see even under his leather getup and silver chains.

Malen proffered his hand and said, "Hi Jamie. It's good to meet you. Haven't been able to get this babbling idiot to shut up about you."

Jamie looked up at Seth in confusion, then back at Malen in time to see the man wink at him in humour. A trickle of amiable energy flowed into him as he shook Malen's hand. It helped to ease some of his wariness and he offered a hesitant smile.

Next came the hairy beast. A full beard stretched from his high cheekbones to the base of his neck where it met tufts of wiry chest hair peeking out from under his flannel shirt. His shaggy, dark brown eyebrows matched his mop of hair, and Jamie was sure his chest was at least three times the width of his own.

Aquene reached out faster than he would have thought a hulking beast could move and grabbed him in a crushing hug, lifting his feet from the floor and spinning him in a circle.

"Ah, my boy! It's about time you showed up in Seth's life to make him whole." Jamie wobbled slightly when Aquene set him back on his feet but the man kept hold of his shoulders and peered down at him. "Wow, you're a pretty little thing. And young. My man's not robbing the cradle, is he?"

Jamie blushed furiously and was grateful when Seth growled and snatched him back against the hardness of his body. "Watch it, old timer, he's mine. And if memory serves right, wasn't Cheryl sixteen when you met her?"

Amazingly, Jamie was able to make out the flush that stained Aquene's cheeks through all of the fuzz on his face. "Still, he can't be more than seventeen, eighteen maybe."

"I'm twenty-two," Jamie bit out in frustration. Would he ever be seen as an adult?

"Easy, baby. He didn't mean any harm. He's just not used to being around someone so small."

Jamie turned a look of disbelief on Seth and jabbed his elbow sharply into the man's gut. If he heard one more insult he was going to kill someone. Seth grunted at the impact and everyone burst into laughter. Everyone except him.

Loland slid into the group and rescued him, taking his hand and pulling him several feet away. He felt a little betrayed by the indulgent smile on his lover's face but at least he wasn't laughing at him or mocking him.

"Don't let these guys get to you. They've had centuries to perfect their stupidity. I'm Jace." The third stranger approached and extended his hand. Jamie looked at it and sighed. Did people always touch this much when they introduced themselves to others? After this onslaught, he didn't want to find out. He was perfectly happy being a hermit.

Jace appeared far less intimidating than the others. He was actually almost the same build as Jamie, but his muscles seemed more defined. His blond hair was shoulder-length and framed an open face. Just before Jamie put his palm in Jace's, he knew. It wasn't a vision, but the new information that flooded him was just as frightening. Jamie let out a startled gasp and jumped back as if avoiding a fire.

"You were hunting him. You wanted to kill him but someone else found him first." Bile rose in his throat as he was assaulted by image after image of the boy's death. The half-breed just like him...who hadn't lived past his sixteenth birthday. "He was burnt and you watched. By the time he finally died, there was nothing left to identify."

No one moved or spoke. The only sound came from the increasingly rapid, ragged breaths he forced from his constricted throat. He couldn't get the picture of the boy's grotesque murder out of his head, or the horrified look of guilt on Jace's face when the man realised afterwards he'd been witness to the death of an innocent.

"You stood by and did nothing. He wasn't just killed, he was tortured. So much pain. You knew it was wrong, but still you let that man draw out his death."

"Jamie, that's enough," Seth warned.

"No, he's right," Jace said. His face had turned to stone and his voice sounded just as devoid of life. "I'll never be able to atone for my failure that night. I came here to...

Shit. I want to help, but…I'll understand if you ask me to leave."

Jamie saw a flash of genuine regret for his mistake of the past in Jace's eyes, but Seth's movement distracted him. Seth walked cautiously over to him as though he was approaching a wild, dangerous animal.

Was he a threat to them? Is that why the other half-God had been so viciously slaughtered…because he deserved to die? He had got the impression of virtue from the boy, but it was so hard to believe that people, and Gods, would want to destroy someone who had done nothing to deserve it. His vision blurred and his cheeks grew warm with moisture.

"Master, I don't want to die. Not like that." His voice cracked. Seth gave up his trepidation and pulled him into a fierce hug.

"You are not going to die," Seth hissed. "Do you hear me? I won't allow it."

"Neither will we," a new voice broke in. As one, all eyes turned to the couple of standing in the doorway to the living room and the men immediately assumed defensive stances. Seth caught Loland's hand and dragged him beside Jamie so that they were both standing at his back behind his protective form.

The energy in Jamie's body changed, drawing into him but remaining near the surface. He was shocked as he watched first Jace, then all three of Seth's friends gather in front of them, ready to risk their lives in the face of the unknown variable this couple of presented.

They could have been twins. The man was a few inches taller than his female companion, but they both shared the same platinum-coloured hair that fell to the small of their backs in straight locks. They were lean, with aristocratic features, and nearly ethereal in their beauty, but what really set them apart was their dress. If ever Jamie had seen a man that fit the part of a Dom, it was the man that stood with an authoritative grace in front of them all. He wore nothing but leathers and held a nonchalant demeanour that spoke of confidence and experience.

The woman wore much the same, with the addition of a flare of lace on her tight shirt and at the hem of her skirt. "I told you, Daddy. Isn't he amazing?"

"Yes, he is," the blond man breathed.

Jamie saw that, unlike the woman, the man was staring at someone other than him. He followed his gaze to the one he'd accused earlier. Jace, that was his name. An unidentifiable current seemed to pass between the two.

The woman let out a peal of laughter. "Well, I was talking about my brother, but you're right too."

"Sir, with all due respect, if you're here to harm my mate, do not expect a welcoming party," Seth spoke.

The blond man took a step forwards and opened his mouth to speak, but the female placed a hand on his chest in placation. "I think it's time I showed them our stand on their—*our*—situation."

The woman closed her eyes and bowed her head, relaxing every muscle in her body as though she were meditating. Static built and the tiny hairs on Jamie's arms and the back of his neck perked up.

All at once, a collective gasp filled the room as a feeling of pure, unadulterated love swept through its occupants and coalesced into an iridescent shimmer that licked over their skin like fire. Energy sizzled in visible sparks that burst in showering displays in the air around them. Passion was like a physical entity that took root in their chests and spread throughout their bodies, infusing every part of their beings with its warmth.

Gradually, the energy dispersed and the feeling of love faded but left a residue that glowed inside each of them. When they were finally able to break the thrall in which they'd been held, Jamie looked around to see confused faces that probably mirrored his own. All except for Aquene's.

"Well doesn't that just tickle my fanny! You're the daughter of Love, aren't you? I always knew that old bat isn't as innocent as she seems." Aquene let out a raucous laugh and strode over to the blond man to shake his hand. "Congratulations, although I have a feeling it's long overdue. Cyaan, right? And this must be your daughter...?"

"Kaia, and please, call me Cy. Your wife sends her regards."

"My wife?" Aquene growled.

Cyaan grinned mischievously, completely unabashed by Aquene's jealous anger. "It seems she's kept a few secrets up her sleeve. She's known about Kaia for quite some time and contacted me a few days ago to let me know about Seth's mate." He turned to Seth then looked straight at Jamie.

"I've had to keep the existence of my daughter hidden for nearly three thousand years now. I had hoped to make our Gods see the error of their ways when I'd heard of the last half-God to exist. Unfortunately, I wasn't able to save him in time. But now, Jamie, you and Kaia have a chance to show them that they would be wrong to condemn you to death simply because you both possess more power than them.

"For all their pride in being above the petty fallibilities of humans, fearing the unknown is one trait they have never been able to conquer. However, the choice is yours, little one. The potential for battle is great, but we will not be without our own strength."

Jamie's head had felt as though it were in a vice, ready to explode with all the new information and possibilities of a situation that already left him feeling lost. But something this stranger had said brought him back to focus. *Little one?* That was Seth's endearment for him and Seth's alone. Hearing it come from the mouth of someone other than his Master diminished its meaning.

Jamie wasn't sure when Seth had come to mean so much to him, but the bruises on his backside, his nickname, the protective look in the man's eyes, they all signified that he belonged to Seth. They let him know that he was cherished and...loved? Maybe, but if nothing else, he was certain that only Seth and Loland had the right to such intimacy with him.

He narrowed his eyes at the presumptuous man before him and said, "Only my Master can call me 'little one'. I'm his, not yours."

The man quirked an eyebrow but it wasn't his reaction Jamie was concerned with. He turned to Seth, expecting to find disapproval over his rudeness, but there was only affection in his eyes. Seth raised a hand and brushed his fingers across Jamie's cheek then circled them around his throat. He tightened them almost imperceptibly. Enough to remind Jamie that Seth held the control, that he would not let him fall.

And just like that, his insecurities disappeared. He finally understood what Loland had tried to explain to him over the past several years. His lover had tried to be dominant for him, but it was nothing compared to the feeling of ownership he received from Seth. It was like coming home.

"You are mine, my little one." Seth held his gaze when another wave of love swept through the room, shocking everyone with its intensity. It was brief but no less passionate than before. Again, all eyes turned to a now bashful Kaia.

"What? I can't help it. I feel love and I have to share it with everyone. It's in my nature."

The strain in the room was broken as Cyaan laughed, joined by the other men. Loland hugged Jamie from behind and as soon as he felt his lover's hard erection press into his sore behind, his own cock swelled and he gasped as his hips involuntarily jerked back. To his utter mortification, he looked up and realised his sudden arousal had not gone unnoticed by Seth or Cyaan. Their knowing looks didn't help matters any.

"I do apologise, Jamie. I meant no offence," Cyaan told him, "but I would still like to know how you feel about what I'm proposing. I believe the time has come to make a stand and let our Gods and the Keepers they influence know that they can no longer sacrifice innocents in the name of their fear. I no more want to endanger you than I do my own daughter, but as she so blatantly made clear to me when we heard of the last half-God, change is necessary.

"If you and your mates choose to hide your existence, I will support that and offer my protection. I do not regret doing the same for Kaia after she was born. But if you choose to challenge the wrongful edict of the Gods, I will do everything within my power to ensure your safety."

Jamie looked at Kaia and saw a strong woman who appeared uninhibited and no worse for wear for her centuries of solitude and secrecy. She was a living example of what his life could be like if he chose caution over defiance. He had a feeling, however, that the shift in energy he had felt when she'd entered the room had more to do with the anguish she held inside rather than the fact that she was a halfling like him.

He'd been catching glimpses of her despair through his precog, but she hid it so well behind her ability to manipulate love, he doubted anyone else was able to detect it. Even her father.

Loland had already been forced to give up two jobs and Seth his time, all in the name of his safety. The idea of inadvertently forcing them to continue to sacrifice their plans and dreams for the sake of his mortality seemed beyond cruel. He knew now that they would never give up on him, but neither could he continue to allow them to abandon everything they'd ever known. He looked into the loving faces of his mates and made his decision.

"We fight."

"Whooo!" Kaia startled everyone with her exclamation and Jamie was pleasingly surprised when he didn't flinch as she flung herself at him, nearly choking the life out of him in her excitement. "Thankyouthankyouthankyou! We can do this, I know we can. Oh, this means we can start on the camping detail. This is going to be so much fun!" she squealed.

"We weren't sure if you would agree to this, so we didn't bring our camping gear, but there must be plenty of stores around here for that. I'll start the phone calls. Daddy, you can ask Seth where the best places to get supplies are. And don't worry 'bout me. Mom said she would chop off the balls of any man who tried to cop a feel. Anyways, I promise to behave in my own little tent among all the sexy, muscular, strong—"

"Kaia…"

" —dutiful and completely honourable men who are about to grace us with their presence." She winked at her father. "Can't blame a girl for checkin' out the goods, though." With that, the white-haired woman skipped out of the room like a teenage girl barely in control of her hormones.

Jamie laughed at the dichotomy of her personality and age but Seth's question caught everyone's attention.

"Camping? If that means more company, I think you'd better explain what's going on, Sir," Seth said, suspicion thick in his voice. Cyaan's answer was cut off, however, by the abrupt departure of Jace. There was no mistaking the anger and stress in his energy, but Jamie got the impression that it was directed inwards and not at any of them in particular. There was also no denying the look of longing on Cyaan's face as he tracked Jace's retreat.

Cyaan's sigh was nearly inaudible as he turned his attention back to Seth. "The Goddess of Love and I have been planning this confrontation ever since we found out she was pregnant with Kaia. We've been waiting for a chance to rally those who recognise and are willing to argue and fight against the injustice of the Gods, but our strength will largely depend on our numbers. I will be able to convince a few Keepers to join us, but the vast majority will be coming because of you."

"Me? Why?" Seth asked.

Cyaan's face broke out into a mischievous grin. "Oh I think I'll wait for you to discover that on your own. There are so few things I find delight in, in my old age, and this surprise is definitely one of them."

* * * *

The next week was chaotic at best and downright exhausting during every waking moment. True to Cyaan's word, Keepers flooded in and filled Seth's extensive lawns with tents, RV's, and campfires. Their reasons for risking their lives and the ire of their Gods varied. Some had been too appalled by the death of the last half-God to sit by and allow it to happen again. Others had been contacted by the mates of Aquene and Malen, or by Cyaan and Kaia.

But most had come because of him.

Seth had assumed his father's legacy after the man had died a few hundred years ago. Not out of a sense of obligation, but because he truly cared for his people, as had his father. Training, he supposed, was akin to giving future generations a firm grasp on their place in the world. It was a responsibility he'd never taken lightly. But to find that so many were willing to show their appreciation for his services by risking themselves both astounded and humbled him.

Loland took to the influx of Keepers like a kid in a candy shop. Seth had been concerned that his mate would be depressed over the fact he'd been forced to give up the job in Vegas, but Loland's energy told him otherwise. The man practically glowed with his eagerness to please him and coordinate the sleeping arrangements and food. Within two days, he'd managed to recruit a small posse who were more than willing to help with the cooking and cleaning.

On the one hand, Seth couldn't blame them for wanting to be around Loland. The amount of energy the man had in volumes was addicting. On the other, he was having more and more difficulty keeping his jealousy in check.

He had prohibited everyone except himself and his mates from entering his bedroom and garden to give Jamie some measure of privacy from the crowds. They'd convinced Jamie that he should also refrain from working until things blew over, but the amount of time that left free for Jamie to dwell on his place in their situation only made him more reclusive.

Fortunately, it seemed Kaia and Jace had taken it upon themselves to help his little one through this. Though Kaia's powers varied considerably from Jamie's, she was undoubtedly the most qualified to train Jamie and teach him control.

Jace's constant companionship was still a mystery. He had no idea what his friend had said to Jamie, but the two were almost inseparable most days. Their current project was the retiling of the inside of the fountain in the garden, and now he found them there arguing over...something.

"You're trying to tap an egg with a sledgehammer. It could take you years at this rate."

Jamie held a hammer and a one-inch-square tile in his hands and growled at Jace. "Oh like you can do better? I've seen the gaps on your side of the fountain. We'll have to redo that whole section."

"Least my tiles are still intact," Jace muttered.

Jamie reached behind him, grabbed the hose and aimed the nozzle at Jace.

"You wouldn't."

Jamie lifted an eyebrow and grinned wickedly. "Keep talkin' shit and I will."

Jace launched himself, tackling Jamie to the ground, trying to wrestle the hose from him. Somewhere in their scuffle, the switch on the nozzle was flipped and water sprayed everywhere.

Seth watched for another minute, caught between wanting to laugh at their playfulness and feeling jealous over their closeness. Finally, he cleared his throat loudly and both men froze to look up at him. By this time, they were completely entangled in the coils of the hose and entirely soaked through.

Seth put on his most stern face but he could have been wearing pink, fluffy bunny slippers for all the good it did him. Jace and Jamie burst into laughter and had to roll over each other several more times to untwist themselves from the hose.

"I can't decide whether finding our mate wrapped around another man is more disturbing or arousing," Loland said from beside him.

"Me either, but damn, he's sexy when he's happy."

"He's happy with you too, you know."

Seth pursed his lips, not knowing what to say to that. That Jamie trusted him and felt more secure around him, he was certain. But with so much going on of late, it had been almost impossible for them to work on their personal relationship, let alone his role as Seth's submissive. Jamie had only just been growing comfortable with asking for what he wanted in Seth as his Dom, and Seth feared this setback might unravel the progress they'd made so far. He made a mental note to rectify that as soon as possible.

Jamie's drenched clothes outlined his slim figure to perfection as he sauntered over and, much to Seth's shock, knelt on the ground only a foot before him. "Master?"

His cock swelled at the sight of his mate's unexpected posture of obedience. Maybe he had been wrong to allow Jamie to slack off from his training as a sub. He hadn't wanted to push the issue for fear of adding to the man's stress, but the subservience he saw now in Jamie's eyes looked as natural as it was gorgeous. He reached down to brush his thumb across Jamie's lips.

"I'm glad to see you're feeling better."

Jamie briefly turned to flick his gaze at the silent form of Jace behind him. "I've been getting some good advice."

Seth glanced in surprise at Jace, who just shrugged his shoulder and gave him a half-grin. He knew his friend was into the lifestyle. They'd done a few scenes together back when they were just fledglings, but that was before the death of the last half-God. Since then, Jace's social life had become all but non-existent. Seth considered himself among the man's closest friends, but even he hardly knew what was going on in his life now.

Come to think of it, the last time he'd seen Jace was shortly after the incident more than three hundred years ago. He'd been only a shell of his former self and had refused to talk about what had happened. The intermittent phone calls they shared kept their friendship alive, but Jace had never fully recovered.

Maybe Jamie wasn't the only one who'd been benefitting from their camaraderie.

"Well, you'll be hearing no complaints from me."

"How are your meetings going?"

Seth grimaced and rubbed his temples. He'd been in conference with the elders in the flock of Keepers since day one, trying to come up with a peaceful solution to their dilemma. After listening to accounts of other half-Gods who had been sacrificed in the name of peace and justice throughout the millennia, he wasn't any more confident than he'd been at the start.

Then again, there had never been this great a congregation of Keepers willing to forcefully change the minds of their Gods.

"We think we may have found a way to get through to the Gods. We're meeting with the Goddess of Love shortly, and I would like for you and Loland to join us. You have just as much a say in all of this as we do." In actuality, it was Jamie and Kaia who would have to agree to the decided plan. After all, it was their lives on the line, but Seth didn't want to put any more pressure on his little one than was absolutely necessary.

"I'll be in my tent if you need anything." Jace made to go around them but Seth stopped him.

"Actually, Cyaan requested that you be there as well."

Jace's face darkened and he opened his mouth but Jamie cut off his retort.

"Please come. I know I have my...mates...but I'd feel better if you were there also. Please?"

Seth felt his breath catch. Was Jamie finally able to accept him as his mate? Hell, if Jace had accomplished that much in the little time he and Jamie had spent together, he wanted the man there too. Seth watched the indecision play across Jace's face. Considering the fact that Jamie's requests and friendships were so rare, it was hard to deny them.

"I need to change, and my tent is at the far edge of the property."

"I can loan you some of my clothes."

Jace raked a hand through his hair and bit his lip. "Guess I don't have much of a choice then."

"Good, it's settled." Jamie bounced up, gave Loland and Seth a quick kiss on the lips, then hauled a queasy-looking Jace through the kitchen and up the stairs.

"Sir, what's up with Jace? Not that I don't like him for keeping Jamie company, but he seems...I don't know...like he's trying to avoid the crowds as much as Jamie is."

Seth sighed. "I don't think he's trying to escape everyone so much as one person in particular." Loland gave him a quizzical look. "I'm not sure myself, boy, but whatever it is, I hope he comes to terms with it before this is all over."

Chapter Eleven

Ten minutes later, they were all gathered in the living room. Jamie sat in between Seth and Loland on the couch. Jace looked as though he were trying to make himself invisible in a corner of the room, and Seth couldn't help but notice that Cyaan couldn't keep his eyes off the man. Kaia was seated next to her father on the loveseat to the side of the couch and Aquene's huge form rested in the recliner. Malen and three elders were in lawn chairs brought in for the purpose of their meetings and scattered in a loosely semi-circle.

"Aquene, why don't you start with what you were able to find out?" Seth said.

The large man looked straight at Jamie, foregoing preliminaries. "I haven't been able to get exact confirmation on whether or not you are the son of the God of Death, but that is the general conclusion we've come to considering your powers. Right after Seth contacted me about you, though, I did discover that Death has another son out there doing his bidding. While you and Kaia are considered brother and sister because of your relation to the Gods, this would be your true brother, if only on your fraternal side.

"We still don't know how it is you came to be raised amongst humans, but your brother is our main concern right now. It seems he is gathering Keepers to him with the promise of power, no doubt fuelled by Death's lies."

"How do you know this?" Jamie asked.

"A friend of mine in New York contacted me. Said he was approached by a group of Keepers claiming they were the subjects of the son of Death—a man called Mikel. They told him that Death would soon have enough power to rule the other Gods and then gave him the option to join them or die."

Seth felt Jamie's body begin to tremble and he pulled his mate further in to his side. "Is he still alive?"

Aquene laughed loudly. "That vicious bugger? Oh, hell yeah. I'm not sure if *they* were by the time he left them, but he's headed here now. He's tough, but from the hints they dropped about their numbers, even he felt it wise to get out of there before they caught up to him again."

Jamie thought for a minute about the implications of what Aquene was saying. "So why hasn't my brother or Death gone through with whatever they're planning yet?"

"The only reason we can think of is that they still need more power from other Keepers, and if you've been having visions of a man hunting you, we think that they may want to use your powers to tip the scales. Each God contains powers that are no more or less than those of their fellow Gods, but if one were to gain access to more, he could, essentially, rule the others."

There was silence as they all waited to gauge Jamie's reaction but it was interrupted by a sudden shower of sparks and streaming ribbons of colour near the doorway to the living room. Jamie and Loland stared wide-eyed as the Goddess of Love made her usual flashy entrance in a gaudy display of fireworks. Once her corporeal being came into focus, Kaia ran to her and their combined squeals were enough to shrivel a man's balls within seconds.

"Oh my goodness, you get lovelier every time I look at you. How are the girls? How is my son-in-law? He hasn't convinced Maimy to chop off her hair, has he? I forgave him for Jesabell, but if he touches one beautiful, golden lock on my baby's head, I'll..."

"Mama! I think he learned his lesson the last time you went after him. Besides, Maimy's not the tomboy her sister is. They're all doing fine back home. When this is over, you'll have to come visit us."

"I will, my darling." The Goddess of Love gave her daughter a kiss on the cheek, then turned to Cyaan to give him an intimate, if modest, hug. Whatever their relationship had been in the past, it was obvious that they now held only fondness for each other. Seth was still trying to wrap his head around the fact that Kaia was mated with kids, a detail that had been left out since meeting her, when he heard a low growl from behind.

He didn't need to look to know that it had come from Jace, but what really intrigued him was Cyaan's reaction. The man appeared...contrite. An emotion he'd never known Cyaan was even capable of. Cyaan took a step towards Jace but must have thought better of it as he swiftly changed directions and resumed his seat. The whole exchange happened in less than ten seconds, long enough to completely confuse Seth, but when he finally glanced at Jace, the man's face was hidden in shadow.

"It's okay, love. I guess I need to work on my boundaries from now on," Love said to Cyaan.

The temptation to ask the triad what it was that Seth had evidently missed was strong, but he held his tongue. The business of personal affairs could come later. "Goddess, thank you for joining us. I take it Cyaan has kept you up to speed on the latest information we've received?" Seth asked.

"He has, and it is quite disturbing. It seems our simple aim to combat the ignorance of my brothers and sisters has become a fight for our very independence. If Death were to gather enough Keepers to pay homage to only him, he could, in theory, gain control over the amount of energy the rest of us receive. We would be dependent upon him for our very existence."

Her words triggered an idea and Seth rushed to say, "If that's the case, then wouldn't the opposite be true? If we could convince enough Keepers to deny him their energy when they send it to the Gods, wouldn't that deplete his power?"

Love thought for a moment then replied, "Yes, I think you're right. Without the energy you gather and give to us, we would lose our capabilities."

One of the elders, Lowell, said, "That would solve our problem with Death, but what about the other Gods? I still don't see how we can make them accept Kaia and Jamie."

"By making them aware of Death's plans and showing them that they have the support of two half-Gods on their side."

"They may try to use this other son of Death as an example. He seems the epitome of everything they try to prevent when they kill a halfling."

"Then we give them no choice," Seth said grimly. "We withhold energy from them just as we will from Death.

They need to be made to realise that half-Gods are no more born evil than the rest of us. One corrupt being should not be the condemning factor for all others of his kind."

"It is possible," Malen chimed in. "We've got one hundred plus Keepers here and more than triple that number if you include their families. Not to mention those that aren't able to travel but are still willing to show their support."

"What should we do about Death's protégé then?" Aquene asked.

Seth looked over at Jamie still huddled against his side. Black bangs had fallen forwards, obscuring his face, but Seth could just make out white teeth worrying at his bottom lip. "What do you think, little one? Aside from Kaia's, your opinion matters the most here."

Jamie didn't answer at first. He raised his head to study each person in the room, though his gaze never stilled on anyone for more than a few seconds. Finally, it came to rest upon Jace's lone figure behind them and stayed there.

Jace returned his stare and Seth could almost feel something pass between them. Whatever silent debate was taking place between the two was apparently decided when Jace nodded his head once and Jamie turned back around in his seat.

With a huff that ruffled his bangs and fanned them out along his cheeks, Jamie said, "We take care of him later. If he's using the promise of power that Death will provide to convince Keepers to side with him, it seems wise to take out the head honcho first and worry about the middle man second."

"I agree," Loland piped up, giving Jamie's hand a squeeze of encouragement.

Kaia nodded her approval and Cyaan's firm voice settled it. "We'll call on the Gods the night after tomorrow to inform them of our decision. Love, please pass the word on to those Gods we know will take our side. We'll need as many in our corner as possible. Meanwhile, we need to find a place to hide Kaia and Jamie. I don't want them there in case anything goes wrong."

"What!?"

"Don't argue with me over this, Kaia. We've been waiting for this for too long to risk anything happening to you or to Jamie."

"He's right," Seth agreed. "I won't take any more chances with the life of my mate than your father will take with yours. It should only be for a few nights and you two will be guarded and kept informed of matters at all times."

Kaia stuck out her bottom lip and turned a pleading look on her mother, but Love just snorted sarcastically. "Girl, don't even go there. I invented that look and you know it doesn't work on me."

Kaia gave up all pretence of indignation and went for petulance instead. It was cute, but not nearly enough to change their minds.

As the meeting came to an end, Seth felt confidence fill him for the first time since learning of his mate's parentage. Come what may, they would get through this with the help of his friends and his kind.

* * * *

Jamie paced the room, studiously ignoring the reproachful look on his lover's face. Loland knelt in front of their closed bedroom door in nothing but a pair of cotton pyjama bottoms, as Seth had requested of them both.

Jamie was dressed similarly but that was as far as he was willing to go to obey. He refused to submit completely to his Master when the man was going to send him away the very next day. It was his life and he should have a say in whether or not he wanted to risk it and stay with his mates during the confrontation with the Gods.

How dare he make that kind of decision for him? Seth had stormed into his life offering love and loyalty and just when Jamie thought he could return those feelings, the man expected him to just stand aside while he faced the danger alone. Maybe not quite alone, but that was beside the point.

Love didn't work that way. Caring for each other meant sticking together through thick and thin, not allowing one to take all of the responsibility. Especially not when that responsibility wasn't even theirs to bear.

Jamie glanced at the clock and noticed only ten minutes had gone by. It seemed like hours since Seth had ordered them to wait for him in the room. Suddenly his powers took mercy on him and he knew he only had one more minute to wait. The realisation made his stomach clench in anticipation and his steps faltered.

"He's coming soon, isn't he?"

"Yes, he is," Jamie replied tightly.

"He's going to be upset if you don't stop pacing and do as he asked."

"I don't care if he's upset. He should be upset. *I'm* upset!"

Loland's knowing grin only spurred him into another round of marching from one end of the room to the other. "You're falling for him, aren't you?"

"He's my Master, isn't he?"

"You know very well that having a Master doesn't equate to being in love."

"Fine," Jamie hissed. Seth was almost to their room and as much as he wanted the man to see his defiance, he didn't want to get his lover in trouble as well. "I care about him, but that doesn't give him the right to..." His words were cut off as the knob turned and Seth's imposing frame filled the doorway.

Jamie sucked in a breath as he was nearly overtaken by the impulse to drop to his knees and lower his eyes. It felt as though he were denying a part of himself in his stubbornness to defy his Master. Two weeks ago, he would have attributed his need to submit to the man to the fact that he was a Dom that Loland trusted, but now... Now he wanted to cede control because it was Seth. *His* Seth, not just Loland's anymore.

Jamie felt his anger waver as Seth quietly closed the door and acknowledged Loland with a gentle caress of his palm under his jaw. He prepared himself for the sharp bite of Seth's commands, questions, fury, anything. But he received none of those.

With bated movements, Seth walked past Jamie without so much as a glance in his direction and continued to the closet where he took down a small, black leather bag from the top shelf. He rummaged through it until he found what he was looking for. Jamie wasn't able to identify the object before Seth enclosed it his large hand, hiding it from sight.

Jamie stiffened as Seth finally met his gaze and walked towards him, desperate to hold on to his rebellion in the face of his Dom's confidence.

"Strip."

Jamie found himself responding to the sheer dominance in that tone before he could think twice about what giving in to that command would signify. He cursed his body's betrayal even as his thumbs hooked under the hem of his pants and pulled them down, displaying his now fully erect cock. He kept his gaze locked with Seth's in an effort to retain some of his insolence, but as soon as he'd kicked away his clothing, his concentration was broken by Seth's firm grip on his member.

His grasp was rough and erotic at the same time. Seth pumped him with hard, unforgiving strokes and Jamie was barely able to suck in a breath before his other hand snaked around his throat.

"You will keep your eyes on me. You want to test your limits? Fine, but you will follow this through to the end."

There was no anger in Seth's energy, but Jamie felt his own return at those words. Then both of Seth's hands increased their pressure and his strokes became brutal, scattering this thoughts. The pace increased until he was brought to the brink of orgasm, and despite all of his defiance, the need to please his Master won out over his own will.

"Please, Sir, I'm going to come. Please... I can't..."

Seth squeezed hard just below the head of his cock and the pain brought tears to his eyes but effectively cut off his impending ejaculation. Jamie was struggling for breath as he watched Seth bend down and quickly attach leather straps around his cock and balls, tightening them until he thought the blood would burst through his skin.

It was almost exactly like the device he'd used on him in the dungeon, but there was a ring on the top of the strap circling his cock that connected to a leash.

Without allowing him to catch his breath, Seth stood and opened the door, tugging on the chain attached to his dick. "Follow us, boy," he said to Loland as he passed by.

Jamie broke out into a cold sweat when he realised his Master meant to lead him through a house full of guests. Naked and trussed up like a willing slave on display. Fear replaced anger and his body froze in place, refusing to acknowledge the painful wrench of the leash. Seth must have registered the terror that had overcome him when he turned back because he showed no hesitation as he drew Jamie into a quelling hug.

"The house is ours tonight. I told everyone that I wanted this time alone to spend with my mates. I would never humiliate or hurt you." He brushed a soft kiss over Jamie's trembling lips. "I'm sorry I worried you, little one. I should have said something sooner."

He tried to regain his earlier temper but was still caught up in his relief over Seth's discretion. The man pivoted and started to lead him again, slowly now, by the leash. Though Jamie trusted him, the knowledge that so many people were camping just beyond the walls of the house kept him on edge for the entire trip to the dungeon.

When they'd entered and Seth had locked the door behind them, a familiar ease settled over him. It was different from what he'd experienced the first time in this room. Then, he had been nervous and a little overwhelmed. Now, he felt just as he did every time he served Seth or lay in his and Loland's arms at night. Comfortable. Safe.

And Seth was sending him away with strangers in the name of his *safety*. As much as he tried to see that as protection, it felt like nothing more than abandonment. He glared at Seth in mute defiance as the man removed the cock leash. If Seth noticed, he never let on. Instead, he walked to the cabinet where he put away the leash and pulled out several other items. He put them on the table to the side then walked towards Jamie with a blindfold in his hand.

"I know you're angry about something, and we'll work that out of you, but you will not disobey me. Since you can't seem to follow the rule of keeping your sight on the ground, we'll have to take it away."

Jamie opened his mouth to argue but Seth reached down and grabbed his balls, slowly closing his fist tighter and tighter until the only sound that escaped Jamie was a whimper. Several seconds passed and he realised he wouldn't be released until he submitted. It was surprisingly easy to do. The complete control that Seth demanded with his eyes, his grip, his huge body corded with muscle, had his cock dripping precum despite the pain.

He closed his mouth and Seth eased his grip until his hand fell away. The blindfold was placed over his eyes, enclosing him in darkness. Panic set in and he raised his hand but it was returned to his side by a firm hand on his wrist.

"I'm right here, baby. I won't leave you. Concentrate on my voice, the noises I make, my touch, heat."

Hot breath fanned across the curve of his neck and he had to clench his fists in order to keep from turning his head to find the mouth he knew was inches from his skin. He was pulled forwards by his hands and stumbled at first, but he could feel Seth's body heat in front of him, soothing him. The air shifted when they came to a stop and he was pushed another step until a horizontal strip of padded leather touched his lower abdomen.

"I want you to bend over and lay your hands above your head. That's it."

Jamie did as told and rested his upper body across more leather. Judging from the size and height, he realised that he must be on the padded table that sat atop a cage large enough for a man to sit in. More leather was wrapped around his wrists and pulled snug, stretching him nicely. Hands caressed his back and sides, sliding down until they neared his groin. His breath hitched, but they didn't stop there. They rubbed his thighs and calves and came to rest at his ankles.

"I'm going to attach a spreader."

Seth nudged his legs until they were at least two feet apart and he felt soft cuffs banded around his ankles. A long metal bar prevented him from closing his legs, exposing his ass to his Master's gaze.

"I want you open to me at all times. Ready for me when I want you. Do you understand?"

If those words didn't clue him in, the fingers that brushed over his quivering hole did. He shivered and his cock grew so hard that he knew, whatever Seth had in store for him, he wouldn't last long.

This would be the first time they would make love together. Always, before now, it had been Loland that Seth commanded to fuck him. Jamie knew that was because Seth wanted to give him time to adjust to their relationship. The idea that the large cock he'd seen plough into Loland's hole was about to take his made him tremble with excitement.

"Come over here, boy."

Jamie knew he was addressing Loland and held his breath as he listened to his lover walk towards them. He heard metal clinking then Seth's fading footsteps. Was he leaving? Was he getting a new toy? He strained to hear what was going on but the rapid beating of his heart filled his ears and masked Seth's whisper-soft movements. Then suddenly he was there again, smoothing his hands over his back and behind.

"I think it's time we broke you in to the flogger you've been wanting. The one I've chosen is soft, but its sting builds." Seth gave a particularly hard squeeze to his left butt cheek. "Are you ready, little one?"

It took him a moment to moisten his mouth enough to say, "Yes Master," but he was still unprepared for the sharp crack of the flogger on his flesh. It startled him more than it hurt, but soon Seth set a light rhythm that he could anticipate, and it calmed him.

As the force of the strokes began to increase, he heard Seth say, "Take him inside of your mouth, boy. Let him feel it but don't let him come."

Jamie was confused until he felt hot wetness surround his cock to the hilt. "Oh fuck!" Strong, sucking pulls ravished him until he was twisting against the cuffs that bound his wrists, desperate to have enough room to move his hips. It was useless though. He was at their mercy and had no choice but to accept what they did to him at their pace. The pain of the lashes and the pleasure of Loland's mouth fused together, holding him in a state of rapture he never wanted to leave.

"Now tell me what has you so angry, little one."

Seth's deep voice broke into his bliss and his mind scrambled to make sense of his words. "W—what?"

Three hard blows, stronger than the others, landed across both cheeks and he sucked in his breath. "Sorry, Sir. I—I..." What the hell had he been mad about? Loland's mouth stilled on his aching member, staving off his orgasm. Seth resumed his rhythm but the strength and pain of the strikes increased.

"I asked you a question."

Pressure was mounting inside him and he struggled against his bonds. The burn of the flogger was beginning to be more than he could handle. *Answer.* He needed to come up with an answer. "You...you want to get rid of me. You're sending me away." More pain. It felt like his skin was on fire.

"You think I'm going to abandon you when this is over?"

There was an edge to Seth's voice Jamie had never heard before. For a brief, horrifying moment, he thought he'd pushed too far. The pain was close to unbearable and still Seth beat the flogger along his back, ass and thighs.

Finally, it came to be too much. Tears stung his eyes and spilled over as he screamed, "Stop. No more. Let me go!" He shook his head from side to side, the pain in his heart rivalling that of his backside. It tore down his defences and brought his fears to the surface. A choking sob wrenched at his chest.

"Tell me what you're afraid of, little one. Talk to me."

He shook his head even harder. The force of the strikes was relentless, crushing the wall he'd put up around his emotions. He felt raw and exposed, teetering on the brink of a cliff. He begged to be released, yelled at his Master, thrashed against the cuffs.

"What do you fear?"

Those words were laced with tender demand, reaching into his soul, devouring him, and they broke him. "I'm afraid you'll leave me!" he screamed. Tears flowed freely now, soaking the blindfold. The renewed suction on his prick both intensified and morphed the sensations in his body. "I'm afraid I'm not worth your love. I'm damaged and I hate it! Please don't make me go away. Please."

"Breathe through it, baby. I'm so proud of you. You have more courage than any man I've ever met. You can do this. Go beyond the pain. Find that place that will let you fly."

Seth continued to praise and urge him, but it wasn't just his words that allowed Jamie to fall into his submissive heaven. It was everything. The constant blows, his tone, the heat of his lover. All of it combined held him in a promise of security. His muscles relaxed and his cries died down while the world fell away. In this moment, there was only him and his two lovers.

"So beautiful. That's it, little one. You please me so much," Seth crooned.

Warmth flooded through him and he felt the blows begin to lessen. He was still floating in a euphoric haze when strong arms lifted and spun him so that he was lying on his back on the leather table top, his wrists twisting in their hold. He wasn't sure how he'd missed Seth releasing the spreader from his ankles so that they could be raised and braced at the backs of his thighs, but it didn't matter. His Master would take care of him.

"Get out and straddle his face while I get him ready, boy. I want your ass right in front of me."

Jamie felt the padding dip as Loland climbed on top of him and pressed his swollen cock to his mouth. He opened immediately and lapped at the fat head, enveloped in his intoxicating scent. Two slicked fingers rubbed his crease then pushed into him at the same time Loland shoved himself further into his mouth. The thrill of being penetrated in both holes had him quivering and moaning and he heard a hiss above him.

Those wonderful fingers forked in and out of his passage, turning and stretching. A third was added and his hips bucked off the table as they curved and hit his sweet spot. He yelled around the hard length, the vibrations from his throat causing Loland to plunge deeper. Every nerve ending in his body fired with each stroke against his nub and he thought he would explode but the sharp cut of Seth's demand stopped him.

"You will not come. I'm not done with you yet."

Jamie whimpered at the loss of the fingers in his ass but he wasn't empty for long. The soft head of Seth's cock slowly pushed in. Once it breached the outer ring, Jamie tensed. It was big, much wider than Loland's cock, and he wasn't sure if he could take it. Memories surged to the surface. Memories of being tied down and forced to take something his body wasn't big enough for. He couldn't pull enough air into his lungs and he fought against his restraints.

"Shhh, breathe, little one. I'm right here. Relax your muscles. You were made for me, remember? Your body was made to fit mine just as I was made to care for it."

Jamie held on to that deep, soothing voice like a lifeline. Hands caressed his belly and his hair as the cock in his ass continued its invasion, but the words didn't stop coming. His breathing eased and when he felt the press of flesh against his buttocks, he knew he'd made it through. Every part of him was so full he felt as though he would burst.

"Very good, baby. Now I want you to count out loud, boy. If you miss one, we're going to start all over again."

He frowned but Seth's meaning soon became clear. He pulled back and slammed into him at the same time he heard a loud slap. Loland's gasp was matched by his and his lover fell forwards, driving himself to the back of Jamie's throat.

"One, Sir."

Another hard thrust and another slap propelled them both forwards and he swallowed more of Loland, sucking greedily.

"Two, Sir."

The burn in his ass blossomed into a pleasure so intense he wanted to beg for his Master to touch him. One squeeze on his dick, more friction—that was all it would take to send him over the edge. He raised his hips and pushed upwards, silently pleading for more, but Seth was having none of it. He held him in a bruising grip with one hand on his hip and set a leisurely but forceful pace. Seth lazily pounded into him, reaching deeper and deeper every time, and Loland's breathless counts quickly turned to shouts.

Jamie grunted with the force of the cocks being shoved down his throat and into his ass. It was too much and not enough all at once. It wrapped him in a sensual cocoon and he could almost see the painful ecstasy on Loland's face through the sounds of his cries. When he reached twenty, Jamie felt his hips being lifted and suddenly the cock that had kept him on the torturous brink pummelled into him. The new angle hit his sweet spot and he circled his legs around wide hips, wanting more, needing more.

Seth was merciless as he ploughed into him, forcing him to surrender everything to his Master. His body shook and his balls drew close as a tingling sensation raced down his spine. He sobbed around the length driving into his mouth, knowing he couldn't last much longer, but he needed his Master's command.

"Come!" Seth shouted.

Jamie's body convulsed and exploded in a blinding shower of white sparks and he flew apart, his screams cut off as he hurriedly tried to swallow the cum shooting down his throat. His ears filled with the combined cries of the men possessing him. Even as Seth continued to hammer into him aggressively, he could feel the pulsing of his mate's cock as his seed spurted into him. He'd never felt so full or complete as he did in that moment.

It took countless seconds for the buzzing energy to settle in his body and for his mind to clear, but even then, he couldn't focus through the haze that clouded his mind. It melted his bones and lulled him until he eventually succumbed, welcoming the darkness with a smile on his lips.

Chapter Twelve

The next day, Jamie found himself sandwiched between Loland and Jace in the back seat of an SUV. He tried to take comfort in his lover's gentle touch, but it didn't diminish the hollow feeling growing in his chest as each mile took him further from the man he'd come to care so much for. That morning, Seth had tended them both. He'd cherished their bodies as he washed them in the shower and kept some part of his body in contact with them at all times.

It had been odd, being on the receiving end of so much blatant need. The role reversal was disconcerting and he hadn't known how to react to it at first. Loland had always been the strong one in their relationship, showing nothing but patience and understanding when Jamie'd had to rely on him to chase the nightmares away.

Then Seth had come, with his implacable will and grounding security. He needed both of them like he needed his next breath, but earlier today, somehow, Jamie had become the provider.

Seth had gathered him into a tight hug, tucking his head into his shoulder and whispering words of reassurance, but something in his tone had made Jamie look up. The longing he'd seen there had robbed him of thought. "I love you, my little one, and I'll never let you go."

He could still feel the aching strain in his heart those words had imbued. And the need to reciprocate them still stuck in his throat, unable to come out. A glance at Loland's face told him he felt the same pang of separation from their mate that Jamie did. Jamie could no longer deny the desire and satisfaction he felt just from being in the man's presence.

The release from his fears that Seth had given him last night, along with the intense pleasure and pain, had solidified Jamie's already growing emotions for him. As soon as it was safe and they could return, he vowed to tell both of his mates how much he appreciated them—loved them.

"Lo?"

"Yeah, baby?"

"Do you want to move in with Seth? When this is over?"

Loland creased his brow and thought for a minute. "I do, but not at the price of losing you. It has to be a choice that both of us make. Do you... Is that something you might want?"

Jamie hesitated. He wanted it—more than he could ever have thought possible. But moving in would mean devoting himself to both men and a D/s relationship, and he wasn't sure if he could live up to their expectations. Seth had described the intense attraction they all felt for each other as the mating pull, and Jamie felt both it and more when he was with his mates. But that didn't mean

Seth wouldn't grow tired of him, as everyone but Loland had in his past.

"We're here," Aquene said from the driver's seat. "We secured it yesterday but let us go in and double-check. We'll be back in just a few." He and the passenger, along with two more Keepers from the Land Rover parked alongside them, got out and headed for the large cabin that Seth owned.

When Jace made to get out as well, Jamie stopped him. "Where are you going?"

His friend nodded towards the passenger side window by Loland. Kaia stood outside looking at them expectantly with a very large Keeper by her side. "I came along to help protect you. All of you. I installed an alarm system last night, but I still need to go over it with the guys. Stay with Kaia for now. It won't take but a few, I promise."

Jamie bit his tongue and slid out with Loland while Jace joined the others. He hadn't wanted to befriend anyone outside his mates, but for some reason, the man had trusted him with a secret no one else knew. The hidden knowledge had allowed him to see a different perspective on life. Seth's perspective. Without it, Jamie wasn't sure he would ever have been able to understand the man's reasons for accepting him and loving him.

Five minutes later, they were waved inside but Jace stayed outside with the other Keepers to show them where he'd put the outdoor cameras.

"Wow, he must have designed and built this cabin and his house," Loland remarked.

Kaia walked ahead and inspected the living room. "How do you know?"

"The layouts are almost identical, except for the lack of a basement and the size."

Jamie looked around and, sure enough, all of the rooms were in the exact locations of those at Seth's house. It wasn't the same, but it was familiar enough to ease some of his angst. The furniture and decorations had a more rustic appeal that blended in with the wilderness outside.

It was only late afternoon, but he felt exhausted with stress over the meeting scheduled for the next night. If one more person tried to reassure him by saying that the Gods were usually very understanding and peaceful, he would rip their lips off and shove them somewhere very unpleasant. He knew nothing of their Gods other than the fact that they would all see him dead if given half the chance. With the exception of Love.

Loland and Kaia were doing their best to keep the mood light and confident, but their optimism just wasn't in Jamie's nature. He knew this was as hard on them as it was on him and decided that seclusion would be better than dragging them along into his depression. Loland had made a beeline to the kitchen, where Jamie found him searching the shelves and fridge. Despite his dark mood, he had to laugh at his lover.

Loland wriggled out from the bottom cabinet he was currently scrutinising and looked up. "What's so funny?"

"You," Jamie chuckled. "It's a wonder we're both not suffering from dunlap disease by now, what with your freaky obsession with cooking and all."

"Dunlap disease?"

"Yeah, where your belly done lapped over your belt."

Loland sat there gaping at him.

"It's a scientifically proven disease. Many people suffer from it. Sad, really." Jace stood in the doorway with the most pathetic sympathetic frown Jamie had ever seen.

"Are you talking about me again?" Aquene came in behind them.

Jace patted the man's considerable gut stretching the limits of his flannel shirt and said, "'Course not. We all know you're nothing but muscle, it just happens to be packed in the area of your stomach."

"Hey, I worked hard at this belly. Not many men can pull this off and still look as sexy as I do."

Jace and Jamie laughed but Loland narrowed his eyes. "I suppose I have you to thank for educating my lover on this 'disease'?"

Jace feigned innocence and slapped his hand over his heart. "Me? I would never."

Loland and Jamie snorted at the same time. "Okay, so I might be a slightly bad influence on him, but you gotta admit, your cooking is irresistible. I've gained three pounds in the past week from it."

"It's true," Aquene chimed in, rubbing his gut. "I've never looked sexier."

Loland pursed his lips but the blush in his cheeks betrayed him. He'd always been a sucker for compliments. The fact that those compliments always held truth was no coincidence. "Yeah, yeah. Butter me up. Now go away. I have dinner to prepare."

Jamie rushed over and gave him a light kiss before Loland really did kick him out of the kitchen. "I'm gonna find us a room and take a nap. Love you."

"You okay, baby? Want me to go with you?"

"I'm fine. Just tired." He could tell by Loland's face that he wasn't falling for his lie, but what was there to say to the truth? Pretty words couldn't take away his anxiety or guilt over the gamble so many people were willing to make for him. He left before Loland could call his bluff and claimed the bedroom at the top of the stairs. The same location as the room he shared with his mates at home.

To his surprise, his and Loland's bags were already there. That must have been Jace's doing. His new friend always seemed uncannily aware of what he needed to feel comfortable. Jamie left them on the floor in front of the dresser, not wanting to unpack. This was only temporary. He would not get cosy because there *would* be a home to return to in a few days. He refused to entertain any other possibility.

He climbed into the king-sized bed and dozed on and off as the rest of the day passed. At some point, Loland had come with a tray of food. Jamie had tried to politely decline the offer, but the conniving little rat was being stubborn. The threat to tell Seth that he'd starved himself during his time away had him shovelling down as much as he could stomach. By Loland's disapproving frown when he was finished, he knew he hadn't eaten as much as he should, but it was the best he could do.

Sleep reclaimed him and, some time later on, the comforting arms of his lover wrapped around his waist and pulled him close. A stuttering sigh was all he could manage before he fell away again.

Then it came.

The vision was unlike any he'd experienced in the past. There was no consumption of his senses. No merging of emotions between him and the people he saw. It was as though he were looking at a future recording, distanced but fully aware of the scene that was playing out before his closed eyes.

A group of ethereal beings stood in a loosely semi-circle in the middle of a field. They appeared majestic and striking. Each one such a study in beauty and perfection, it was almost hard to look upon them.

A short distance in front of them massed the band of Keepers who had rallied to Seth's cause. They stood proud yet humble, each one nodding his or her head in deference to their Gods. Silence reigned and the moment seemed rife with apprehension. They were waiting for something, but Jamie didn't know what.

Then the front of the crowd parted and Seth walked forwards. He stopped halfway between the groups and bowed slightly to the Gods. His mouth opened and his lips began to move but no sound came out.

That's when Jamie realised the deafening silence was not because no one spoke, but because the noise was withheld from him.

He was distracted from the oddity of that when the Gods all took one step forwards. Their countenances transformed from serenity to outrage in the blink of an eye. Their lips curled up into snarls and their teeth were bared as they shouted at Seth, then at the assembly of Keepers behind him. Jamie wanted to warn Seth. To tell him to run. Seth's life was worth more than the chance he was taking, but it was too late.

Fire erupted from the hands of the Gods and, when they raised them, shot out towards the crowd. Spitting waves of orange and blue flames flowed along the ground, eating away the distance at a rapid pace. Within seconds, it had reached Seth and licked its way greedily up his trousers. Moments later, the waves crashed upon the other Keepers, clinging to them no matter how far they ran or rolled in their attempts to douse the fire.

By the time Jamie looked back to Seth, there was nothing but a living wall of flame where the Keepers had been. Jamie saw a look of utter defeat and despair in the beautiful silver eyes of his mate before the fire roared up and consumed him completely. He didn't writhe or run, but just stood there, a pillar of flame, as though he accepted his fate.

Jamie jerked upright and caught his breath in time to stifle the sob clawing its way from his chest. His body was hot and tight, as thought the flames had been dancing along his skin just moments ago, but a glance down revealed only rivulets of sweat and flushed skin.

When he closed his lids, he could still see the devastation of his vision. The desolation in Seth's eyes as he realised that he'd not only died for nothing, but so had the people who'd supported him.

Jamie had felt none of their emotions like he usually did in his visions, but he was grateful for that anomaly. His own were raging so far beyond his control that more would have sent him over the edge. Desperation finally won out over grief and his mind scrambled to come up with a plan. His visions always came true, but for once, he wasn't going to prepare for the outcome—he was going to prevent it. He had to. Even if it meant his own death.

Jamie took several deep breaths to centre himself, but when he quietly got out of the bed, he couldn't stop the tremors that racked him. Fear was alive in him, its stench coating his nostrils and clogging his throat. He stumbled to the adjoining bathroom but avoided looking at his reflection in the large mirror. He didn't want to see the horror he knew was in his eyes. The same horror that had blazed in the eyes of the mass of Keepers at Seth's back.

He quickly wet a washcloth and wiped the sweat from his body, foregoing a shower for fear of waking Loland. By the time he was dressed with his duffle in hand, he still had no clue of a plan, but that could come later. For now, he had to leave.

There was still time. The meeting with the Gods was scheduled to take place tomorrow night... A glance at the digital clock on the nightstand told him it was after one in the morning. Okay then, tonight. But that still gave him several hours to think of something.

He peered down at Loland's face, so peaceful in his slumber. Even asleep, the corners of his mouth were curved up, as though his sunny personality was preparing for the joy of the next day. Jamie didn't have to memorise his features. They were so far engrained in his mind that they had become a part of his very existence.

Tears welled but he blinked them away and slipped out of the room without a sound. Years of learning to hide his presence from unwanted attention held him in good stead as he crept down the stairs and to the foyer.

He grabbed the keys to the SUV from a hook on the wall and headed for the back door in the kitchen. Aquene had taken the Land Rover back to join Seth. He silently thanked Jace's insistence that he know the code to the alarm system in case of an emergency.

Two sequences of four digits disabled it and he passed through the doorway, making sure to enable the alarm again once he was out. A cool breeze whipped his hair into his face and he cursed himself for not remembering his jacket, but the car lay just around the corner in front of the cabin. He strode swiftly over the grass but froze when he heard a voice behind him.

"Going somewhere?"

Jamie's heart beat frantically as he spun around to confront the stranger. Only he wasn't a stranger. Relief flooded him as he took in the stoic form of Jace. It only lasted a mere second though before suspicion replaced it. Had his friend been expecting him to run in the middle of the night?

"I have to leave. I…I saw something. A vision. What are you doing out here?"

"I was keeping watch. That and I couldn't sleep. Are you trying to go back to Seth?"

Jamie shook his head with a little too much emphasis and Jace's eyes narrowed. "I just have to get out of here. If you try to stop me, I'll only find another way. There's something I have to do."

Jace's brow wrinkled and he stared at him for several heartbeats. Jamie held his breath. He didn't want to fight with his friend, but he would if it came down to it. Lives were at stake, all in his name, and there was no way he was going to sit by and let the future he'd seen play out.

Jace must have sensed his resolve, because his face relaxed into resignation. "Did you get the keys to the car?"

Jamie nodded.

"But no coat, huh?" His lips quirked up in a lopsided grin.

Blood rushed to his cheeks and he shrugged. "Spur of the moment thing and all that. Are you going to let me go?"

"No. I'm coming with you." Jace pulled off the windbreaker he was wearing and handed it over. "Put this on. It'll take the car a while to heat up. And give me the keys. You don't look like you should be driving right now."

"What? Wait. No, no, no. You can't come with me. I don't even know what I'm going to do yet."

"Well then, we'll just have to think of something on the way. Seth told me about that little trick Loland pulled with the handcuffs right before I met you. Don't think I'm above doing the same thing if it means keeping you safe. I may be as small as you but I've definitely got more muscle."

Jamie growled in frustration. What was it with men and their egos? Always out to protect someone for their greater good by any means necessary.

And wasn't he just the pot calling the kettle black?

Well, damn.

With another growl, he handed over the keys and pulled on the jacket.

He would have argued that Jace needed it more being as how he'd probably been out here for hours, but he was well accustomed to his friend's level of stubbornness, having a good measure of his own.

Jace grinned triumphantly but had the good sense to try to hide it as he took Jamie's bag and headed to the SUV. It was a newer model, so the engine turned over with a low purr. It would take them a while to get to the main road and thoughts of how he was going to change the massacre to come flitted through his head until it pounded mercilessly. He knew he was still in shock, but he was running on a very restricted time limit.

"So are you going to tell me about this vision you had?"

Jace's question broke into his thoughts and he sighed, giving up on them for now. "You're not going to like it," he warned.

"I kinda figured that. Tell me anyways."

The pain and terror Jamie felt earlier had resided into a dull ache as he allowed his shock to numb everything inside. At first, he didn't think he could talk about it, but the images were still fresh in his mind and he had a feeling a few hours wouldn't lessen their impact.

"My vision...it wasn't like the others I've had. It was different. Felt different. I can't explain it, but they've always come true in the past." He paused. Jace waited patiently, giving him time to regain his composure. He stared out of the window and continued. "I saw the meeting they're going to have with the Gods tonight. Everything started out well. Seth stepped forwards to speak to them. I couldn't hear what he said. Usually every sense I have is attuned to my visions, but not this time.

"They began arguing. The Gods were furious. And then..." Jamie's throat choked around the next words. "Then they spouted fire from their hands. It spread so quickly. It was everywhere." A single tear escaped but he brushed it away, anger seeping in to replace the numbness. "There was no escape. They killed them, Jace. Everyone. But my Master... Seth—he was the last to die. He looked so..." Jamie clenched his fists and glared at the man next to him, though his rage was directed elsewhere. "I can't let that happen. I don't care what I have to do, but I can't let so many innocent people sacrifice their lives for mine."

The darkness in the car hid most of Jace's expression from him, but from what he could see, his face showed nothing. His only indication that Jace was bothered by what he'd just heard was the death grip he had upon the steering wheel. Jamie thought he could hear the protest of the plastic beneath his hands.

They rode in silence for several minutes, this time to allow Jace the chance to recover himself. Jamie knew he was probably reliving his own past. The coincidence that the vision had shown the Keepers' deaths by fire, the same manner in which the last half-God had died, was too much to ignore.

"So what do you want to do now?" Jace's voice was rough, almost a whisper.

"I know this has to be hard for you. You don't need to help."

Though the shadows concealed his features, when Jace finally looked at him, his emotions were evident in his tone. "Has it ever occurred to you that I'm helping you because I like you? Yes, I failed my mate when he died at the hand of Wrath. I should have discovered him and protected him before it was too late. And while I saw coming here as an opportunity to make up for my mistake, it's not why I'm in this car with you right now. Your being a half-God just like my mate was no longer matters. I'm here as your friend, and I'm going to help you whether you like it or not."

Jamie laughed reluctantly. Those words didn't take away his guilt over putting the man in danger, but they went a long way towards allaying some of his fears. "Okay then. Can we stop at a hotel for a few? I have no idea what our next move should be and my brain's a little too fried to think about it right now."

"Sure, just let me get a few hours down the road. I don't want Seth to kill me before we get a chance to save his ass."

Jamie chuckled and settled further into his seat but didn't bother closing his eyes. He was going to have nightmares for the rest of his life about that vision, however long that turned out to be.

They travelled in silence, both too immersed in their own thoughts to keep a conversation going. By the time they reached a small town a little more than a hundred miles away, Jamie made Jace pull into a hotel on the outskirts. It wasn't as far as they wanted to get, but his friend was sagging in his seat and looked exhausted. Jamie couldn't imagine he'd got more than just a few hours sleep in the past two days, what with securing the cabin and standing guard outside at o'dark early in the morning.

Amazingly, Jaime felt himself dragging as well despite the severity of the situation. Emotional stress always took a greater toll on him than physical stress. Jace checked them in with cash using a false name and as soon as they got to the room, they flopped onto the queen beds with relish.

"I am entirely too wiped to take a shower. It's all yours if you want it," Jace said.

"Nah. I'm not even sure if I have the energy to strip and get under these covers."

Jace grinned at him. "You sleep in the nude too? Would you mind if I did? I can't stand it when my clothes bunch up every time I roll over."

Jamie was already unbuttoning his pants and wriggling free of them while lying down. "No problem. 'Course I don't think my mates need to hear about it, but it's all gravy to me."

They were both down to their boxers and under the blankets in seconds flat. The bed was a relief after the confinement of the car, but it was big and devoid of the extra bodies he'd grown accustomed to being squished between. The bruises that still marred his backside from Seth's attention were a warm reminder of the men he loved, but it wasn't enough to stave off his loneliness.

He listened to see if Jace's breathing had slowed but it sounded the same to him. "Jace?"

"What's up?"

"I don't mean to sound kinky or nothing but do you...suppose that maybe you could..."

"Jamie, you can ask me anything. What's on your mind?"

This was definitely easier to say in his head. He rushed out the words before he could think twice. "Would you mind getting in bed with me? I haven't slept alone since Lo got me out of...well, a bad place. I miss him, and Seth, but I trust you. I just don't want to be alone right now."

He held his breath, waiting for a rejection, but he should have known better. Jace threw back his covers and climbed into bed with him. He moulded the front of his body to Jamie's back and stretched his arm around his stomach. He was no larger than Jamie, but his touch was sure and soft and full of soothing energy.

"Is that better?"

"Yeah. That's a lot better. Thank you, Jace."

"Anytime."

Chapter Thirteen

Jamie's eyes fluttered open and blinked in the darkness. There was no sunlight tinting the windows or sounds of cars and people outside. The thought occurred to him that they might have slept the entire day away but he just as quickly dismissed it. They'd set the alarm clock and to this day, he had never been able to sleep through one. The noise they made grated on his nerves too much.

Jace was still pressed against him but slept as quietly as he usually was while awake. Jamie concentrated on his hearing, trying to discover what had wakened him. Then he heard it. Boot heels clicked on the pavement outside their hotel room door and he knew who it was a moment before it opened and several large figures swarmed in. The room exploded into chaos and Jace was ripped away. Jamie flung himself to the floor on the other side of the bed.

Jace's shout was muffled by a hand over his mouth and three men fell on him like vultures. Jamie darted to the side, trying to use his small size to get around them, but there were too many. He managed to land a shot to the groin on one guy but another punched him in the back of the head and the force of it thrust him into the arms of a third. The pain stunned him long enough for them to bind his wrists and ankles. His scream was cut off by a strip of duct tape and a terrifying pressure at his throat.

Out of the corner of his eye, he saw another assailant hoist an unconscious Jace over one shoulder and carry him out of the room. He fought for all he was worth, but he was no match for them. The man who'd bound him lifted him effortlessly, but he was still able to get in a good kick to the other in front of them. Arms crushed him to a massive chest and squeezed until his next breath became more important than his freedom.

A low voice hissed in his ear, "I was told not to damage you, but if you don't stop fighting, I'm going to show your little boyfriend what a real man is made of."

And the battle was won. He could deal with what they dished out to him, but he could not allow his friend to suffer needlessly. Once he grew still, the man threw him over his shoulder and headed out to the parking lot. He saw the men who'd taken Jace climbing into a Suburban before he was shoved into the back of a similar vehicle.

It was big enough to seat at least eight or nine people but the third row of seats must have been taken out, judging by the amount of room he had to move in. A mesh grate separated him from the men who sat down in the first two rows.

The car jolted roughly when the driver put it into motion and he tumbled against the back doors, banging his already throbbing head. He tried to keep track of the twists and turns they made, but the trip was long and the driver no more merciful than he'd been from the start.

He was shivering, bruised and sore by the time the vehicle came to a stop. Bright morning light spilled in when they opened the doors, temporarily blinding him. He shied away but they hauled him out.

One man covered his head with a loosely black hood that was tied into place around his neck. The sensory deprivation combined with fatigue caused him to stumble more than walk. He heard one of them grumble something unintelligible before he was thrown over another shoulder.

Jamie found it ironic that for the first time in his life, he wanted to rebel against what was being done to him, but he couldn't. He was responsible for Jace's safety. Again, another role reversal, but if it meant saving his friend from harm, he was all for it.

The hood cut off most of his oxygen and his full bladder protested with every step, but he remained docile. He knew that the man stalking him in his dreams was the same one who had set this up. The sooner he met with him, the sooner he could bargain to get a message to Seth to cancel the meeting. He wasn't sure if his disappearance would be enough to halt the coming disaster.

He lost track of time again and was brought out of his reverie when he was swung down and his back hit a cold, stone floor. The air rushed from his lungs but before he could recuperate, the men made quick work of him. The rope around his wrists and ankles were cut and what felt like a heavy, iron shackle was attached to one ankle. The hood and tape covering his mouth came off next. Before he had a chance to form a question, they'd filed out of the room.

It took a few minutes for his eyes to adjust. There were slim cracks outlining the only door that let in just enough light for him to discern his surroundings. The metal clasping his ankle was new, along with the chain and plate that bolted it to the wall behind him. There were more chains and manacles hanging to his side. Apparently they didn't see him as that much of a threat. Not that he could blame them.

What little else there was in the room was rusted and covered in layers of dirt and grime. An aluminium bucket was in the corner beside him and there was a high, square window positioned a few feet from the ceiling in the wall on his other side. At least, at one time it had been a window. Steel bars barricaded it along with wooden planks behind them, effectively eliminating both sunlight and any chance of escape via that route.

Jamie rose on weak legs and relieved himself in the bucket, then pushed it as far away from him as possible while still retaining access to it. His revulsion at being reduced to no more than a captive animal was great, but he had more important things to worry about. It was hard to focus his mind, though, when he couldn't get past his concern for Jace.

A short time later, he heard shuffling outside, then the door was opened and Jace was thrown inside. He was still tied in the same manner Jamie had been, but he fought wildly. Jamie stood to help but one of the men anticipated his move and tucked an arm around his neck, applying pressure until he could only claw at it.

Jace got in a few kicks but he was swiftly overwhelmed by three of the men. A fourth untied his wrists and shackled them both, along with his ankles. Another was placed around his neck with a much shorter chain. The fourth man punched him so hard that his skull cracked against the hard floor beneath him and his body went limp. They retreated from the room again and as soon as Jamie was freed, he rushed over to Jace.

"How sweet. I've never been mated myself, but I hear it's quite the thrill."

Jamie whipped his head around at the sound of the deep, syrupy voice and felt his blood run cold. It was him. The man who had invaded his dreams. The one from his vision. He had the same raven-coloured hair and black, soulless eyes. The energy around Jamie shifted just as it did when he was in Kaia's presence, but there was a distinct malevolence that shrouded this man. His black clothes suited his heart, Jamie thought.

"What, no joy at finally meeting your long lost brother?"

"What do you want with us?" Jamie's courage was strengthened when his voice came out hard and low, disguising the fear that clutched at his gut.

Mikel narrowed his eyes and peered down at him as though he were an insect being dissected. "You don't seem surprised by that statement. In fact, I'd venture to say that you've been expecting me."

Jace sat up beside him and glared at the man but remained silent.

"I've seen you in my dreams. I've known you've been hunting me for months now."

"Interesting." A sick glow of excitement flickered in his eyes. "I'd heard you have visions. Did you enjoy the one I sent you last night? It took me a while to get the images just right. I've never met your other mate, Seth, but I've gleaned pictures of him from the minds of others. Quite handsome, actually." His eyes strayed to Jace's rigid form. "You've done very well for yourself."

Jamie's mind struggled to understand the meaning of his words. "You...you sent that vision to me? It wasn't real?"

The man laughed maniacally. "Of course not, but it was good, wasn't it? How else was I to get you away from all of those Keepers without implicating myself? I can't have a war until I'm fully prepared for it and you, my brother, are going to help me."

Dread rivalled the anger in him at being so easily manipulated. He should have known, or at least consulted Loland. The vision had been different, but he'd been so caught up in his own fears that he hadn't stopped to consider those differences, or what they might have meant.

"Our father wanted you dead after he couldn't find you, but I convinced him to let me use you. However, I need your compliance for that. Side with me and I promise to stay away from your precious Seth."

Jamie's head span with alarm for his mates. He couldn't stand the thought of Seth or Loland being hurt at the hands of this madman. On the other hand, if he willingly used his powers to aid him in his quest to control Gods and Keepers alike, there was no telling how many would suffer because of him.

"Jamie, don't." Jace's voice broke him from his swirling thoughts, and he looked into his friend's adamant, hazel gaze. "Seth is strong, with the force of an army of Keepers at his back. Believe in him. Don't let this asshole convince you otherwise. If he had the power to hurt him, he would have done so by now."

He was right. Seth had never shown anything but strength and wisdom. If Jamie had stayed and told him about the odd vision, they wouldn't be in this mess right now. With firm resolve, he looked back at the man and said, "No. I won't help you. My mate will find a way to get us out of here."

Annoyance blazed briefly in his eyes but disappeared as they settled once again on Jace. A slow smile cracked his stern façade and Jamie flinched at the lust he saw in them. "Fine. I suppose one mate is as good as another. Let's see how you feel after I'm done with him." He pivoted and yelled for his men to take Jace.

Confusion clouded his mind until the man's meaning finally registered. "Wait, he's not my mate. Take me. He's nobody."

He was raked with a condescending sneer. "Don't insult me. I know you have two mates. Do you expect me to believe that you would be in bed naked with another man if he wasn't one of your mates? I was told he was human, but this works just as well."

The same men who had brought Jace in appeared in the doorway. Jamie looked to his friend and saw his face pale.

"Would you like me to show you my other gift, brother?"

One of the guards tackled him and pulled him to one side of the room in the same neck embrace he'd been held in before. He watched in horror as Mikel knelt close to Jace while another began to unlock his cuffs. Unlike earlier, there was no fight or resistance. Jace simply stared straight ahead, eyes unfocussed and body pliant.

"You will do as I command, is that clear?"

"Yes, sir."

Jace's voice sounded drugged and distant. Once the chains fell away, he sluggishly complied with the order to stand and follow their captor.

"No!" Jamie screamed. "Take me, please! Leave him alone. He has nothing to do with this."

"Then tell me what your other powers are. Join me and I will release him."

Jamie wanted to. Not knowing what was in store for Jace had his imagination running wild. But he had to believe that they would get through this. He had to have faith in those he trusted.

His brother must have seen his decision but instead of the frustration he expected, he saw victory and desire. It didn't add up until he followed his gaze to Jace's nearly nude body. Like a puppet, Jace followed the man out of the room, and even after the guard left and he was alone, Jamie screamed until his voice gave out.

* * * *

The explosive sound of glass shattering had Cyaan and Seth racing to the kitchen. His mate was in there, and with the stress of the past several days riding him, he was ready to rip apart anyone who would dare go after Loland. The sight that met him, however, was almost worse. Splinters of glass littered the floor and the steaming casserole Loland had been baking lay all around his bare feet. On his feet.

Seth narrowly dodged the ceramic sugar pot that flew past his head before crashing into the wall behind him, and reached Loland in time to save the next object his mate grabbed. He lifted him up but nearly lost him again as Loland flailed his arms and legs, fighting him the entire way to the downstairs bathroom.

"Let me down! Let me go, please Sir. I can't do this anymore! I can't...I can't just wait here. Please, I have to..."

"Shhh, baby. I know."

"No, you don't know!" Loland squirmed in his arms and pushed at his chest, trying to get free. "I promised I would always take care of him and I failed. I failed in the hospital and I failed when that crazy asshole hurt him to get to me."

Seth sat him on the countertop beside the sink, inserting himself between his legs. When Loland reared back, he caught his head just before it smashed into the mirror behind him. "Enough! You are not responsible for this. Do you hear me?"

"The fuck I'm not! I was holding him in my arms and I still lost him. And what are you doing about it aside from sitting on your... "

Seth absorbed all of Loland's violent energy into himself, leaving nothing behind, and Loland promptly passed out. He knew his mate had been bottling his emotions up until this point, but the force of his guilt and anger mixed with his own was like a blow to his psyche. He would have to release the energy soon, but Loland's care came first.

He gently stripped him down and assessed his injuries. Loland was wearing nothing but pants, which had protected his legs but his feet were red and raw from the hot food, with tiny slivers of glass coating them. A few of his fingertips were also blistered but thankfully that was all he could find. After stripping him, Seth ran cool water from the sink over his feet, making sure to remove the shards before patting them dry.

With a curse, he recalled that the burn ointment he kept for emergencies was in the bathroom upstairs and the nearest towels were in a closet in the hallway outside. He was about to strip out of his own shirt to cover Loland's nudity when there was a knock on the door. He laid Loland's limp body in the dry tub then turned to see who it was. Cyaan stood there, with a robe in one hand and the tube of ointment in the other.

Seth gave him a grim smile and took the items. "Thanks, man." Once his mate was medicated and bundled, he carried him to their room and took the robe off before tucking him under the covers. A wave of shame hit him as he took in the dark circles under Loland's eyes and the stress lines on his brow and around his lips. Even in sleep, his mate's agony over their loss was plain to see.

"Don't take this onto yourself. The time for self-recrimination can come later," Cyaan said from the doorway. If it had been anyone else intruding on his privacy with Loland, he would not have been able to hold back his temper. But Cyaan was his friend, former Dom, and teacher. And the man seemed to be suffering just as much as he was.

The Gods had had no choice but to accept Kaia. The fact that she was mated with children and had lived peacefully for thousands of years attested to her good nature. They would have been fools to label her a threat simply because of her additional powers. But they withheld their judgement on Jamie, demanding proof that he wasn't a threat either. That was impossible to do, however, without Jamie's actual presence.

After they'd concluded that either Death or Mikel had Jamie and Jace, the warriors amongst the Keepers who had come to offer their support stayed in order to help him recover his lost mate and friend. It had quickly become obvious to Seth, however, that Cyaan was taking all of this just as personally as he was.

"You're right. I appreciate that you stayed here with the others to help, but something tells me there's more to it than that."

Cyaan pressed his lips into a thin line and his body tensed. Indecision warred on his face and for the first time since Seth had met the ancient, his composure lacked its usual air of confidence. "He's my mate. Jace," he clarified.

Seth almost staggered back at the news. His mind reeled but it came up blank. "Does he know? Did you know before now? If Fate screwed around with you too... "

"No. She told me when he became my mate, but that wasn't until after...after Jace got over what happened to him."

Again he felt nothing but confusion. "Maybe you'd better start from the beginning."

Cyaan sighed and dragged a hand through his white locks. "Maybe I should. I don't plan on letting him go after we find them. Mind if we talk about this somewhere a little more comfortable? And preferably with a stiff drink in our hands?"

"Sure." He led the way down to his study and poured them both a few fingers of whisky from the crystal decanter on the shelf beside his desk. They sat opposite each other on twin recliners and Seth waited for his friend to continue.

"Fate came to tell me that Jace was my mate just hours before I heard about your Jamie. When I asked her why she'd taken so long to let me know I had another mate, she said that the boy who died, the half-God that Wrath killed, was Jace's first mate. As you know, it's not uncommon for us to find a second mate if our first dies. I've had two others in my lifetime.

"Well, after the boy's death, he wasn't in the right frame of mind to accept another mate. I don't understand why it took him over three hundred years to come to terms with it, but apparently, by his deciding to help you protect Jamie, Fate felt that he was ready. I approached him after I got here, but he was...less than enthusiastic about the idea."

"Oh Gods. I knew he was devastated over the murder but I thought it was because his father had pressured him into killing an innocent."

"His father?"

"Yeah. You didn't know? That man's a real piece of work. Told Jace that he had to prove himself a man by being the one to kill the halfling. I thought he was mad at himself for realising that he'd been about to kill a child in the name of his father's twisted sense of honour."

Seth grimaced. "I wouldn't put it past his old man to be the one that prevented him from moving on. I told Jace he needed to cut ties with him but I guess that never happened. Wait...if Jace didn't find out that that boy was his mate until Wrath killed him, then that means that Fate had denied him the knowledge just as she denied me."

"Hmm. I think it's time we had a little talk with the Goddess."

"So do I."

They both downed the contents of their glasses then walked out to Seth's garden. The sun was setting but there was still plenty of light illuminating the foliage and trees. Forgoing preliminaries, Seth shouted out, "Fate! Get your ass down here now." Cyaan stood to his side and they both watched as the Goddess materialised on the stone bench in front of them.

An ugly sneer marred her flawless features but it was nothing less than what he expected from her. "Don't you dare yell at me like that. I agreed to give your mutts a chance just like the rest of the Gods, but don't push it."

"Mutts?" Cyaan growled.

"Our edict to the Gods was real, Fate. Not a bluff," Seth interrupted. "And it includes you. So unless you want to go hunting for your ration of energy elsewhere, I suggest you give us the information you've been hiding."

She tightened her blue eyes and stubbornly crossed her arms over her chest. Seth could just make out the telltale flush in her cheeks. She never had been good at subterfuge. "I have no idea what you're talking about. Now, if you're done wasting my time… "

"We know who has Jamie and Jace, as I'm sure you know too. My first question is how do you know?"

She crossed her legs and huffed, the fine peach-coloured silks that barely covered her shapely figure fluttering in the slight breeze. "You don't have to get all pissy about it. I suppose there's no point in keeping his dirty little secret now anyway. I didn't know about Mikel until after I found out about Jamie."

"Death's other son?" Cyaan asked.

"His first son. Mikel's mother chose to stay with Death and help him with his plans. The little tramp actually loves him, if that's even possible. Anyway, Jamie's mom came later but she wasn't exactly what you'd call a willing participant. She was fated to mate with another Keeper but when I tracked her down, she was already pregnant with Jamie and being held prisoner by Death."

"He forced this woman to have his baby?" With all that was going on, Seth wasn't sure why the thought of a God committing rape amazed him so, but it did.

"Well, he forced her to get pregnant with his child, but apparently she wanted her baby. I thought maybe I could take her to her mate after she had it but when I went back for her, she was gone. Death, the lazy bastard, had grown complacent and she escaped his guards right before she gave birth."

"So she gave Jamie to humans to raise in order to hide him from Death?"

"She must have, though I didn't know it at the time. Death eventually found her and killed her but she never told him what she did with the baby. He promised me that he would track him down and either use him or kill him."

"Then why did you try to keep me from Loland if you thought Jamie was out of the picture?"

"Because I didn't *know* he was taken care of. Death never gave me a definitive answer and I didn't want to take the chance that you would find out."

Seth shared an incredulous look with Cyaan. So many lives altered and ruined and Fate spoke of them as if they were mere inconveniences on her part. "Did you even think to tell anyone what was going on? What Death was planning?"

"Of course," she snapped. "It's not exactly like I relish the idea of serving my brother, but you Keepers aren't the only ones who can suffer at the hands of the Gods. We can hurt each other just as easily, and I'm sorry, but I happen to like my existence as is. Now, that's really all I know, so if you don't mind... "

Seth could see her start to fade but he wasn't done quite yet. "Wait. Tell us where to find Jamie and Jace. If you were able to sense Jamie's mother while she was in Death's custody, then you should be able to sense them too."

This time, a spark of true regret lit her eyes, but it was too little too late. "I can't. I've tried. I'm not completely heartless, but either Death or Mikel are cloaking them from me. And before you ask, I have no idea how they're doing it. It's beyond my capabilities to reverse." And with that, she was gone.

The rage on Cyaan's face reflected his own. Despite what they had just learned, they were still right back where they'd started. "So what do we do now?"

"I think I might have an idea."

Both men turned to the voice behind them.

"Kaia, I thought I told you to return to your family. The Gods may have accepted you but it's still not safe here," Cyaan admonished.

Kaia walked to her father and cupped his cheek in her hand. "Daddy, I'm just as much my mother's daughter as I am yours. I can feel your love for your mate, and your pain. Did you really think I could sit by if there was something I could do to help?"

"I'll not have you in harm's way."

She smiled, and it lit up the garden more than the fading rays of the sun. "Don't worry. If I'm right, I can help and give you guys all the glory of riding in to the rescue."

A shred of hope bloomed in Seth's chest for the first time since hearing about the disappearance of his mate. "What are you proposing?"

"I'm assuming you know that Jamie's ability to absorb energy extends far beyond the range of any mere Keeper, as does mine. When I sense love, I also sense the strength of its energy. Jamie's is very unique. His love carries so many emotions that I have no doubt I'll be able to feel it no matter how far away he is."

"But?"

She hesitated now and chewed on a thumbnail. "But...I won't be able to sense his energy until he releases it. When he was in this garden, he gave his loving energy to the plants and it was an awesome thing to feel. If he can do that again, wherever he is, I have no doubt I'll recognise it and should be able to pinpoint his location from there. Have you talked to him about being able to do that yet?"

His chest deflated and hope wisped away as quickly as it had come. "No. I haven't trained him at all. I was so concerned with getting him to love me and accept our relationship. Fuck!"

"Seth, this is more than what we had to go on previously," Cyaan said in a low voice. "Jamie will eventually have to release his energy, so it's a guarantee. We just need to wait until then."

"And pray that he releases enough of it at once for Kaia to detect? If he's being held away from nature, that may never happen."

All three stared at each other in mute grimness. The plan was out of their control and far from ideal, but it was all they had at the moment.

Chapter Fourteen

Jamie waited for them to arrive, both anticipating and dreading it. It was how he measured the days. Every evening — or morning, he knew not which since they never let him leave his cell — he was given a hard chunk of bread and some water. Every day he tried to save some for his friend, and every day they found it and took it before returning Jace.

The periods during which his brother, Mikel, removed Jace were lengthening. At first, it had only been for a few hours a day. Now, Jamie was lucky to spend a few hours with him before they hauled him off again.

The worst part was watching his helpless compliance each time Mikel came for him. He'd discovered his brother could control the minds of Keepers and humans, but not Gods or half-Gods. Jace's unwilling subservience was as horrifying to look upon as the lashes and bruises that covered him each time they brought him back.

The lock on the outside of the door clicked and light spilled in from the hallway. Two men carried Jace in by his arms, too weak to walk on his own. They shackled his wrists, ankles and neck and left him curled into a ball on the floor. Mikel strode in once the guards left and grinned at Jamie maliciously.

"Have you had a change of heart yet?"

Jamie only glared at him in defiance. It was the same question Mikel asked him each day upon Jace's return. He'd learnt better than to be goaded into conversations with him. Mikel had an answer for every one of his rebuttals, but the logic he used was so twisted that it was useless to argue with him.

"No? That's all right. It will still be several more months, maybe years, before my army of Keepers is strong enough to take control of the Gods. I have plenty of time to convince you. Meanwhile, I'm having entirely too much fun with my new pet."

Mikel crouched down beside Jace and stroked his hair in a deceptively loving manner. His friend trembled violently but didn't make a sound.

"Get away from him," Jamie hissed. He wanted to rip the offending hand from Jace's body, to tear his brother limb from limb, but he knew the guards were still outside. The moment he advanced on Mikel, they would beat him unconscious, just as they had the last time he'd tried. He'd only made that mistake once, but that didn't lessen the temptation.

"You know, I was never into men. Didn't see the appeal. Still don't, to tell the truth. But I have to admit, your mate is better than any woman I've bedded. Pretty, for a man. And the way he submits... "

Jamie swallowed the bile rising from his stomach. "You're killing him. You think I'm going to join you when he's dead?"

"Oh, I won't let him die. I can promise you that. Hell, I almost regret needing you at all. Nothing would please me more than to keep him as my permanent pet." He grabbed a fistful of hair and wrenched Jace's head up. "Would you like that, boy?"

Blood dribbled from his lips, and when he opened them more poured out. His throat worked convulsively but all he could manage was a slight nod. His sunken lids remained closed and when Mikel released him, he huddled back into himself. Jamie fought against the tears stinging his eyes.

He knew what it was to be defenceless. Forced to obey the will of one stronger and more ruthless. He wasn't sure whether it was better to be the observer or the victim, though. Both positions seemed to hold the same amount of pain.

Mikel stood and faced him again. "I'll be back for him in an hour. We have new Keepers to welcome into our family and your mate provides such wonderful entertainment."

"You sick, nasty, perverted son of a bitch!"

Mikel drew back one foot and kicked the side of Jace's ribs so hard his back and skull struck the wall with a sickening thud. More blood flew from his mouth and Jamie's vision turned red at the sight. He threw himself at the larger man and got in as many blows as he could before the guards pulled him off. He went down after a blinding shot to his left temple, but Mikel stopped them from causing further damage.

"Leave him. Hatred is good for the soul. Besides, I want him to see his mate when we're done with him tonight. Or tomorrow."

Jamie jumped back up and flung himself at his brother but he was already gone. The cuff around his ankle yanked him back and he braced his hands to break his fall. In all of his life, he had never had the courage to stand up to a larger man, but then, he had never been responsible for the pain of another either. His defiance both amazed and disgusted him. He was proud that he was trying to defend himself and Jace, but it wasn't nearly enough.

Ignoring the pain in his head, he crawled over to where Jace had crumpled and took a closer look at his wounds. The skin that wasn't coated in dried or fresh blood was coloured with bruises in various stages of healing. His blond hair hung in clumps, hiding the edges of his face that he couldn't conceal under his arms. Jamie moved to gather him into his lap but Jace shied away from his touch.

The tears he'd been holding in broke free and fell silently down his cheeks. "Jace, please." His voice broke and he had to clear his throat to start again. "Let me just tell him what he wants to hear. Once you're free, you can tell Seth where I am."

It was the same plea he made every time they dragged Jace back, and his friend answered it with the same stubbornness as always. Jace unfurled himself slowly, as though he might break with sudden movement, and fixed his hazel gaze on him. His eyes were dark now — as green as the algae that floated in the depths of the ocean and filled with pain just as deep.

"No," he croaked. "Wai for Sheth."

"Oh God." Jamie reached out without thinking, grabbing onto his lower jaw and inserting two fingers into his mouth to pry it open. Jace flinched and let out a gargled protest but Jamie didn't let go. What he saw inside brought on a fresh wave of tears. Little puncture wounds dotted the top of Jace's tongue, the insides of his cheeks and the roof of his mouth. Each was the size of a dog's canine and when he looked to the sides of his lips, his suspicion was confirmed.

He'd read about spiked ball gags during his research into BDSM, but those had originated as torture devices and were not accepted in the average BDSM community, if at all. When he pulled his fingers from Jace's mouth, they were almost completely red. Jace sank back down to his prone position and buried his face in his knees.

Another glance over his friend's shaking form set his resolve. As Mikel had told him, it would take a lot of time for him to gather his forces, but it was time that Jace didn't have. Already, his muscles had lost their definition and his belly was caved in on itself. Jamie hadn't seen him eat once since they'd been captured and Jace refused to tell him whether Mikel fed him or not. He refused to talk about anything that happened outside their cell.

Jamie would bluff his way into his brother's confidences until he was sure Jace was free and pray that Seth found him in time to stop his brother's demented plans. For now, he offered what little comfort he could to the man who sacrificed so much for him. He reached out again and Jace whimpered at his light touch, but it was the only way he knew to transfer energy.

Placing his palms gently over Jace's lacerated back, he leant down and started humming a soothing lullaby while he gathered the energy in his body. He thought of Seth's garden and the freedom he had gained from having the vitality of so much plant life coursing through his veins and dancing along his flesh. He didn't have those resources with him now, but he wanted them so badly. He wanted to give Jace a brief respite from the madness and the pain.

Then, it came. More energy than he knew his body contained seeped into his being like the warm rays of the sun they had been denied for too long. But it was different, tainted somehow. Lacking the purity of nature. He likened it to the rare times he'd absorbed negative energy from Loland.

Was it possible that he was pulling energy from the Keepers who held them? If so, it was also possible that he could transform it, mould it to his will. It was something he'd been forced to learn long ago on his own. Negative energy had killed the plants he'd tried to release it to. But by infusing a measure of his own positivity, he could give life. Health.

He did so now. It wasn't much. He was holding on to hope by his nails, but Jace deserved everything he had. It converged within him in a slowly spiralling vortex that gradually lightened and gained speed. Without faltering in his hushed song, he allowed the energy to flow into Jace.

There was resistance at first and Jamie opened his eyes to look down at his friend. He met surprise with patience and continued to push until he felt Jace's acceptance of what he offered. Then it was like the floodgates of a dam had cracked open. Energy burst like wildfire through him and he used the love he felt for his mates to alter the enmity it contained.

Jamie was rewarded for his efforts when Jace laid his head in his lap and sighed. No smile curled his lips and the lines of stress that creased his brow remained, but there was solace. Jace slept without nightmares until they came for him again.

* * * *

Jamie jerked awake to the sounds of fighting. Shouts and crashes resounded off the walls beyond his cell as he shook away the fog of sleep. Adrenaline coursed through him, making his depleted stomach feel queasy and his hands shake. This was the first time he'd heard any commotion outside his prison and hope flared that it was Seth and the other Keepers come to rescue them. But he quashed it.

He couldn't afford the depression he would feel if it turned out to be a simple brawl among Mikel's followers. Crawling as close to the door as his chain would allow him, he lay on his belly and tried to make out the words being yelled. It was no use. If anything, the noises began to fade as though the battle was being taken further from him.

He craned his neck, desperate to know what was going on, but the sudden slam of a large object against the door had him rearing back. Shuffling feet were silhouetted along the bottom seam of the door. More crashes sounded, but this time there was the unmistakable crunch of fists meeting flesh and bone.

Fear flooded him and he cringed back to the wall on the opposite side. If this was an inner dispute between Mikel's men, there was nothing to stop one of them from entering his cell and taking advantage of the chaos. Jamie held his breath and listened as the fighting stopped in the hallway. Whoever was left standing raced away.

Several seconds passed and he almost jumped when he heard someone shout, "Jamie! Jace!" His heart pounded furiously in his chest. He knew that voice. It wasn't the one that had filled his dreams and thoughts this past week, but it was still sweet music to his ears.

"Right here. I'm in here!" More footsteps outside, then that voice again.

"Jamie?" The man rapped on the door.

"Yes. It's me."

"Stand away from the door and cover your face."

He instantly obeyed and a moment later, the heavy wooden door and frame shattered inwards under the force of the man's boot. Splinters and chunks flew and he waited for the debris to settle before looking up. Cyaan's tall, imposing, frightening frame was the best sight he'd seen in too long.

"Thank the Gods you're alive. Are you hurt?"

Jamie knew what Cyaan saw when he trailed his scrutinising gaze over his body. They hadn't allowed him to bathe or dress and lack of food made his skin gaunt on his already thin frame. Bruises and scrapes lay under the layer of dirt covering him from his beating, but he knew he looked like a finely groomed, healthy young man compared to Jace.

"I'm fine. I'm chained to the wall, though." He pointed to his ankle where the bracelet chafed at raw skin. Cyaan leant down to peer at it, then at the wall mount it was attached to. It seemed hard to believe that just days ago, he would have drawn back in fear at having such a large man kneel so close to him. Now, it made his heart hammer in gratitude.

"I'm afraid this is reinforced. Too strong for me to break on my own. I'm going to need you to give me some of your energy."

Jamie shook his head. "I gave it all to Jace. He was... I was trying to help him." Some emotion he couldn't name flickered in Cyaan's eyes, then he blinked and it was gone.

"You can pull it from the life all around you, at great distances. You did it last night. It's how Kaia was able to locate you. I know it probably exhausted you, but I need you to try once again. Just give me a little bit and I'll take care of the rest."

Jamie couldn't quite understand what he meant, but the distant sounds of fighting were increasing in volume. Not wanting to waste any more precious time, he repeated the process he'd gone through in the garden and earlier with Jace. Just as before, energy flowed into him, invigorating him. When he placed a hand on Cyaan's bare arm, it jumped and sparked as Jamie released it.

There was a loud clang and then he was draped in Cyaan's shirt and lifted into his arms. His ankle ached and he longed to massage it, but a glance down showed that it was free of its shackle. That was enough for now.

"Come on. Let's get you out of here. We're not far from the front entrance."

When Cyaan turned and headed out of the cell, Jamie noticed for the first time that two other Keepers had been guarding the door, watching for Mikel's men. Appreciation washed over him and the anticipation of finally seeing Seth again was powerful, but something wasn't right.

"Wait," he said to Cyaan's bare chest. He was jostled against its broadness as they ascended a set of stairs, the two fellow Keepers close behind them. "Wait," he repeated, this time looking up into the man's hard face. They ran down another corridor and Jamie began to struggle in his hold. "I can't leave yet. Let me down."

His impatience grew as he was thoroughly ignored. Growling, he bit down hard on Cyaan's biceps and yelped when he was abruptly dropped to his feet. An arm whipped around his waist to keep him upright.

"Mind telling me the reason for that?"

Cyaan's impatience matched his, which only served to agitate Jamie further. "We have to find Jace. We can't leave him in here."

"I will, but I need to get you out of here first."

"No. I can feel him. His energy. It would take you too long to search for him on your own." He was beginning to grasp the vast difference between his Keeper powers and those of the others. Cyaan hadn't been able to sense that Jamie was in the very cell he was fighting outside, but Jamie had no such limitations. He could detect the signature of Jace's energy like the flame of a candle in the dark.

"It's too dangerous in here for you. I won't risk your welfare any more than I would that of my ma...Jace. We don't have time for this. Now let's go."

The evidence of Jace's suffering at the hands of his brother, all to keep him unharmed, flashed through his mind. It wasn't courage or valour or anything of the sort that convinced him Jace was more important than the threat of danger to him. Jace was his friend. Jamie had never known friendship outside what he had with Loland, and now Seth. He found it was something he cherished more than his own well-being.

He twisted away from Cyaan's tightening hold and gave his stubbornness full rein. "I am not leaving here without him. Either you come with, or I'm going alone."

Cyaan's jaw flexed and Jamie could feel his irritation, but his resolve was implacable. Relief expelled the breath he hadn't known he'd been holding when the larger man nodded his head in acquiescence.

He'd had a lot of time to become familiar with Jace's unique thread of energy these past several days. Its greatest distinction lay in the fact that Jace had so much pent-up anxiety and pain. Feeling him was like clutching at a live wire. His agony of late had become almost too much for Jamie to bear, and when he searched for his friend's energy now, it bowled into him with sickening force.

Strong hands steadied him as his body wavered under the onslaught, but he pushed them away and headed in the direction that would lead them to Jace. "I'm okay. He's upstairs somewhere. We were blindfolded when they brought us in. Do you know how many floors this building has?"

"Five, including the basement where we found you," Cyaan replied.

Jamie nodded. "Then he'll be on the top floor. I'll lead the way once you get us there."

No more words were needed and they all rushed through long hallways and expansive rooms. They ran into the occasional Keeper turned rogue, or rather, groups of twos or threes. Cyaan and his men made quick work of them, and even though Jamie took that time to catch his breath, his muscles were screaming before they made it to the top. Inertia and starvation had weakened him more than he'd thought.

Halfway up the last stretch of stairs, he faltered and would have done a face-plant if not for the quick reflexes of the man behind him. Beefy arms had scooped him up and adjusted him next to an equally burly chest by the time Cyaan noticed and span around.

With a self-deprecating curse, he reached his arms out for Jamie. "I'm sorry, I wasn't thinking."

"I've got him. You can be the hero for the next sexy man in distress." The dark-haired giant who had Jamie tucked effortlessly in his arms winked down at him. Laughter bubbled up, easing some of his discomfort at being held so intimately for the second time in the last hour by a virtual stranger.

Cyaan didn't smile, but his thankfulness was written all over his face. "Can you still sense him?"

Jamie pointed to an oak door at the end of the hall once they reached the top floor and Cyaan took off. Burly Man quickened his pace once he heard Cyaan gasp at whatever he saw in the room. It wasn't obvious at first. The room was huge and filled with gaudy tapestries and opulent furniture. A four-poster bed dominated the centre with strips of gauze creating a halo around it. There was no doubt in Jamie's mind that this was Mikel's bedroom.

Cyaan ran to a far corner that was cloaked in shadow and it was then that he saw his friend. A standing cage was suspended from the ceiling by a thick chain. Another, thinner chain led from its roof on the inside to a pair of manacles attached to Jace's wrists. His head sagged back in unconsciousness and his feet barely touched the base. More bruises and open wounds covered his body, and what Jamie assumed was the spiked ball gag forced his mouth wide.

Black rage unlike any Jamie had ever seen contorted Cyaan's face, but it was with a steady hand that he unhooked the latch on the door and reached in to wake Jace. The smaller man jolted as soon as he felt the touch on his neck. His eyes stretched wide in fear and his whimpers were cut off as he swallowed convulsively.

"Shhh, it's okay love," Cyaan crooned. "I won't hurt you. I would never hurt you. You're safe now. We're going to get you out of here, but I need you to be still. Can you do that?"

The cage rattled with the force of Jace's trembling and he flinched when his face was cradled by two gentle hands, but Cyaan never let up. "Look at me. I am not him. I am your mate. You will calm yourself for me. I'm going to remove this gag so you can breathe, but do not move. I don't want you injured further."

After the sick dominance Mikel had forced onto Jace over the past week, Jamie didn't think more domination was the best approach. He wriggled out of burly man's arms and walked over to them, ready to offer what support he could. By the time he got to them, however, it wasn't necessary. They had locked gazes and whatever passed between them seemed to pull Jace out of his panic attack.

As soon as Jace nodded, Cyaan unbuckled the strap wrapped around his head. Blood trickled from the corners of his mouth before he clamped it shut and swallowed repeatedly. Jamie took the last few steps to them and laid his fingers on Cyaan's arm. Energy swirled inside him and he channelled it into the man until Jace's cuffs broke apart in Cyaan's grip. Swiftly, he stood back as Cyaan lifted Jace before his body collapsed to the floor.

"All right. Jamie, let Chris take you again. We're not far from the back exit but we still have three flights of stairs to go down. Once we get there, I want you and Jace to stay in the car Loland is waiting inside until Seth and I come back for you. No matter what happens, you are to stay put."

The stern look to enforce his words was not needed. As soon as he heard that Loland was waiting for him outside, Jaime leapt into Burly Man's arms and nodded excitedly. He didn't like the idea of sitting by while Seth and the others endangered themselves, but he knew he was far too weak to help. Besides, he didn't want to leave Jace alone just yet.

The third Keeper stripped off his shirt and handed it to Cyaan who, with his help, managed to pull it over Jace's naked form without letting him go. It amazed Jamie to see his friend cling to Cyaan with such trust. As far as he knew, Jace had become almost as much of a recluse as Jamie since the death of his mate.

Mate. Cyaan's earlier words finally registered and his jaw dropped. Was it possible that Cyaan was Jace's mate? Did Keepers get another chance at a mate?

They were running back the way they had come before Jamie could ask any of his questions. The only opposing Keepers they came across were either lying unconscious on the floor or too injured to attack. Until they got outside.

The bright, morning sun blinded him and he landed hard on packed earth in a heap of tangled limbs. The Keeper who'd struck Chris charged without hesitation. Jaime was shoved away just in time to avoid being trapped between the two and he blinked his eyes rapidly to help them adjust. Fortunately, the Keeper was far more interested in taking down Chris than he was in him. Unfortunately, a watery glance showed him that their small rescue party was severely outnumbered.

Cyaan suffered a sharp punch to the ribs while he was setting Jace on the ground. Four men swarmed him but he launched into his defence and drove them away as soon as he turned around. The fluidity and grace with which he fought was captivating, but his split attention gave the others an advantage. Jamie quickly saw that the four were merely a decoy. A fifth was closing in on Jace, but collapsed under Cyaan's fist. That earned him another slam to his back.

"Jamie, take Jace and run!" Cyaan shouted.

Jamie stood and dodged several attempts at him until he reached his friend. "Can you move?" Jace nodded and rose to his feet with his help. He knew they had to get around to the front of the building but they were boxed in on both sides by men fighting. In front of them lay a vast expanse of desert interspersed with scraggly bushes, cacti, and still more men fighting.

He pulled one of Jace's arms over his shoulders and headed towards a dried riverbed that looked like it offered a little cover, but the going was slow. It was hard to distinguish who was friend or foe so they avoided everyone. He tried desperately to find Seth among the mass of combatants but he was nowhere to be seen.

Just as they reached the edge, Jace was yanked away from behind while a steel grip fell on Jamie's neck. He spun to meet the crazed look in his brother's eyes.

"Didn't think you would get away from me that easily, did you?" Mikel sneered. He definitely looked worse for wear. A heavy layer of dust filmed his hair and clothes and there was dried blood on his bottom lip and knuckles. Jamie reared back his fist but Mikel was quicker. He ducked the punch to his jaw and backhanded him so hard, blood sprayed from his nose and lips.

Jace tackled Mikel a split second later and they all landed on the ground. The breath was brutally knocked from Jamie's lungs and he looked up in time to see his brother roll away and slam Jace's head into the dirt.

"Jamie!"

Jamie and Mikel turned to see Seth racing towards them but he was still quite a distance away.

Mikel grabbed hold of his wrist and shouted, "Father!" Suddenly, a man appeared out of thin air to their right. He looked the exact duplicate of Mikel, but a trimmed beard and moustache hid half of his face. His black eyes were cold and calculating and a look of disdain contorted his handsome features.

"I told you to kill him."

"His powers will be of use to me. Get us out of here and I can still prove it to you."

Death raised his hand and pointed it at them but three other figures appeared behind him.

"This comes to an end now, Death," A tall man with auburn hair spoke. "Give us your sons before we are forced to exact full punishment."

"Your punishment will be nothing once Mikel carries through with my demands." Death brought his hand up once again and, just as sparks coloured his fingertips, Jace leaned over and bit down hard on Mikel's ear. His hold on Jamie's wrist loosened just enough for him to wrest out of it and roll away. A searing flash of light preceded a loud scream that was cut off abruptly.

The energy was drained from Jamie's body and he slipped away into darkness.

Chapter Fifteen

A disorienting, vacuous wave swept through the field of combatants, sucking the energy from them until the only ones left standing were the trio of Gods. The sudden silence in its wake was deafening. Seth stayed on his knees through sheer force of will, as did Cyaan and a few others.

The Goddess of Love surveyed the damage with abhorrence until her eyes settled on her former lover. "Time, give those who still serve us back their energy, unless you want to clean up this mess yourself."

The Gods of Time and Vengeance looked equally disgusted as they took in the carnage. "I think we should decide where to put the rebels first," Vengeance said.

"This isn't the first time in history we've had an uprising due to the overzealousness of one of us. Maybe we should open the doors of the Vishian again."

Time narrowed his gaze at Love. "If we do that, we'll need to recruit Keepers to guard them there."

"True, but it won't be for long. Once they realise their leader will remain incapacitated indefinitely, they will give up their devotion to him and his quest for more power. Now, release their energy."

Time looked less than convinced, but he bowed his head in acquiescence and said, "Very well. I'll begin the preparations with the other Gods." With a flick of his wrist, Seth felt energy return to his body in a rush. Time and Vengeance vanished, but his only concern was for the small man lying unconscious on the ground near Love.

He jumped to his feet and ran the remaining ten yards to his mate. Jamie wore nothing but a dirty pair of boxers and a T-shirt that came down to his knees. There were no serious injuries that he could find. Purple bruises circled his eyes as though he hadn't slept in too long and he appeared even more fragile than usual. Seth gathered him onto his lap and wept in joy for the strong pulse he felt along his neck.

He rocked him and peppered kisses all over his face. The sight of Jamie in Mikel's grasp with Death poised to blast them played over and over in his mind. Despite all of their well-laid plans for this rescue mission, it had all come down to the courage of Jace and Jamie.

"Jace?"

Seth followed the gruff voice to the stoic form of Cyaan several feet away.

"I am so sorry, my love." Love took a step towards him but the look he sent stopped her.

"Is he..." Cyaan cleared his throat. "Is he dead?"

Love slowly shook her head. "I don't believe so. Death used his powers to teleport Jace and Mikel somewhere right before Time drained him. It took a while to convince my brothers and sisters to help once Kaia gained Jamie's location. Then it took longer for us to infuse enough of our energy into Time so that he could contain Death's powers. We got here as soon as we could."

"But not soon enough. Mikel still has my mate and we have no way of finding him." Cyaan's tortured gaze fell on Jamie's limp body.

"He saved him, you know," Seth said. "If Jace hadn't distracted Mikel right before the blast, he would have them both right now. I am in your mate's debt, and I won't stop helping you until we find him."

Love reached her hand out to Cyaan then let it drop. The man's grief blazed in his eyes, inconsolable. Seth knew from recent experience that no amount of words or gestures could soothe the pain of knowing that a loved one, a *mate,* was suffering. Cyaan nodded to both of them then turned to walk away. Seth didn't try to stop him.

"Take your mates and go," Love said. "I'll find Aquene and organise the cleanup crew and the relocation of these poor fools."

Seth nodded. "Thank you for everything. And please give your daughter my gratitude. I owe her just as much." He wiped the tears from his eyes and stood with Jamie in his arms. Heading towards his car, he noted with grim satisfaction that the majority of casualties had been taken on the enemies' side.

Loland was standing by the passenger door and ran at full speed once he caught sight of them. "Is he okay? What happened? Is he hurt? Let me have him. I have to hold him."

"Calm, boy. He's fine, just exhausted like you are. Let me put him in the back seat and you can hold him for the entire trip home."

Loland span on his heel and climbed into the car, making impatient gestures with his hands by the time Seth got there. He chuckled and very carefully laid Jamie down with his head in Loland's lap, then got behind the wheel. He didn't want to let go of his other mate now that he had him back, but he settled for listening to Loland talk and sing quietly to him.

The drive was more than seven hours, and though he was relieved to have the ugly business with Mikel over, there was still one other concern with which to occupy his mind. Jamie had been subjected to the worst of Keepers and Gods alike, right upon his introduction to them, no less. He'd been hunted, kidnapped, forced to face the possibility of death by the very Gods Seth served, and made to do who-knew-what by his own brother and father.

And behind it all was Seth's failure. He'd insisted that his mates hide with Kaia, even after Jamie had begged him not to send him away. It had been a poor judgement call that had cost the man undue pain…and was still costing Jace if he yet lived. Jamie would be well within his rights to demand Seth stay away from him, and Loland would go as well.

After what had happened, he would rather be without both mates just to know that Jamie would never be alone again.

It wouldn't be the end of their relationship, but there was no telling how long it would take him to gain forgiveness and another chance, even from Loland. Since Jamie's disappearance, his boy had grown increasingly despondent and quiet. He'd leaned on Seth as a Dom, but avoided all talk of emotions.

Thoughts and doubts swirled, and by the time they reached his house, he felt no less stressed than he had that morning. He parked and opened the back seat door, looking down at his two sleeping mates. With a soft caress, he woke Loland and whispered, "We're home. Do you mind if I carry him inside?"

Loland yawned drowsily. "Sure. He's still asleep, though. Maybe there's something wrong we didn't notice before."

"Not asleep," Jamie said groggily. He blinked open his crystal blue eyes and stared straight at Seth. "Carry me, please."

Seth tried to put on his best smile, but knew he didn't quite succeed. The idea of living for eternity without that needful expression directed at him was almost more than he could take.

"With pleasure." After Loland got out, he bundled Jamie against his chest and took him inside. He figured it would be quite some time before the others returned to pack up their stuff and say goodbye. For now, they had the house to themselves.

Loland walked ahead and turned down the covers to their bed so he could tuck Jamie in.

"No. I need a shower. I feel so dirty."

Those words triggered something deadly in Seth. He sat Jamie down on the edge of the bed and asked, "Mikel didn't...did he...force you to... " He couldn't finish the sentence.

Large tears gathered in Jamie's eyes and he shook his head. In a tiny voice, he said, "No. That was Jace. Mikel took control of his mind, made him submit to his will, but not me. He thought Jace was my mate, so he...hurt him to get to me. I should have done something but Jace kept telling me to wait for you. That you would come for us. Is he okay now? Where is he?"

Seth took a shuddering breath. He didn't want to answer that. It would only give Jamie further cause to hate him, but he deserved the truth. "Mikel was teleported by Death to an unknown location just before the other Gods could stop him. He was holding on to you and Jace, but Jace distracted him long enough for you to get away. I think because Jace was still touching Mikel, he was teleported as well."

"You mean Jace is still with him? Somewhere?"

Seth nodded.

"Then we have to find him. You found us before."

"I'm sorry, little one. We were able to find you because of your powers. Cyaan and I will never stop looking for him. We just need another plan."

"You don't understand!" Jamie jumped up and grabbed onto his hand, imploring with his eyes. "You don't know what he did to him. Jace won't survive that much longer. He did it all to protect me. We have to find him."

Seth pulled him into a fierce embrace. "All right baby. We'll all work together to get him back."

"Me too," Loland said. "Don't forget me."

Seth chuckled and pulled his other mate to them. "Never. Now let me get that bath started. I want you two naked and ready in ten minutes." He left them alone and closed the door to the bathroom, giving them some privacy. After starting the water, he found the candles and bubble bath Kaia had given him to celebrate Jamie's homecoming. He'd thought it a bit pre-emptive and corny at the time, though now he could have kissed her for it.

When everything was ready, he turned off the lights, allowing the soft glow of candlelight to fill the room, then opened the door to check on his mates.

He froze in shock. Both knelt before him in beautiful poses of submission. Their hands were held behind their backs with their heads held high and eyes lowered. Even Jamie's pain over the loss of his friend was subdued.

"What is this?"

The two shared a covert glance then Jamie said, "I don't want to be away from you again. I love you. You and Loland. I want you to be my Master and my mate. I know I ran away when I should have trusted you, and I promise never to do it again, but I'm yours…if you still want me."

The heartfelt longing in his tone drove Seth to his knees. He cupped his hands under both men's chins, raising them until he could look them in the eye. "I love you, too, and I will always want you. Both of you, but I need you for life. As my subs, my mates, my lovers. Will you accept me?"

"Does this mean I get full access to the garden?" Jamie asked.

"And the kitchen?" Loland piped up.

"And the books in the study?"

"Oh! And decorating privileges?"

Seth threw back his head and laughed — truly laughed for the first time in what seemed like years. "Yes, anything you want. Now get your asses in the tub before I have to punish them."

The evil glint in their eyes only made him laugh harder.

About the Author

Nicky McCoy has always been a lover of books, particularly those with the dichotomy of the strong alpha male and the weaker love of their life which they must rescue. After reading all she could find in M/F books, she decided to give M/M fiction a try and her addiction skyrocketed.

Hot, sexy men times two? No contest. Unfortunately, Nicky was reading faster than the authors could produce. Eventually, she resorted to imagining her own stories and her mind took off from there.

She has to admit, though, she is a bit of a recluse. If not for the joy and humour her husband and four boys bring to her, she would never have ventured this far.

Nikki McCoy loves to hear from readers. You can find her contact information, website details and author profile page at http://www.total-e-bound.com

Total-E-Bound Publishing

www.total-e-bound.com

Take a look at our exciting range of literagasmic™
erotic romance titles and discover pure quality
at Total-E-Bound.